BLUEJAY

MEGAN STOCKTON

D & T
PUBLISHING

When I was just a few chapters into Bluejay, I had the immense pleasure of being invited to a writing group by fellow author and horror lover Peter Marsh (P.R. Marsh). This group consisted of such an amazing collection of individuals and I was so intimidated by the quality of their work. I told them I was writing a little novella where I would play along the line of extreme horror, but I wanted to maintain my typical style with character-driven storytelling. They were so supportive and encouraging, I really don't know if I would have had the confidence to submit this to a publisher without them. So to Peter Marsh, Joshua MacMillan, Gage Greenwood, and Jae Mazer... Thank you so much for giving me the courage I needed. I think D&T will do better with this release than I ever could have on my own.

On that note, I want to thank Dawn for taking a chance on me and giving me the opportunity to work with her and her amazing team.

I also want to thank my sister, Morgan, who has been my horror co-pilot and reading buddy for my entire life. No matter what I send her, she always buckles down and reads it and provides feedback. She lets me spout off ideas and talk about the most ridiculous story details any time of the day. Without her I would have crumbled a long time ago.

1

EVERY MORNING NOAH noticed he was balding. It was like a surprise; he'd walk by the mirror on his way to take a piss and do a double take at the guy with the receding hairline in the looking glass. Sometimes he'd use his palm to shield seeing himself there, like seeing someone at a party that he was trying to avoid. Soon, he'd have more hair on his face than his head. He wasn't old enough to be balding, was he? Then he'd realize that he wasn't young anymore, either.

He didn't *accept it*, but the thought crossed his mind.

He put on his glasses and a blue, holey bathrobe and a pair of ridiculous house shoes. He made coffee, mixing so much caramel and half-and-half that he could've convinced you that it didn't contain any coffee at all. He put it into a mug that read 'World's Greatest Dad' and retrieved a curly pink straw from a drawer. It's worth mentioning that Noah didn't have any children that he knew of. After burning his upper lip when he tested the coffee from the side of the mug for the appropriate temperature, he added a few ice cubes and stirred feverishly.

Noah then collapsed into his computer chair, booting up the massive rig. He didn't even game anymore, but he had an emotional attachment to the computer and refused to sell it for something more portable and practical. Fans kicked on almost immediately, and he could feel the warmth of the old machine heating his ankles. His cat came to the source of heat, rubbing against his bare legs underneath his robe with a trill.

He didn't have to work today, and so his favorite pastime was being a keyboard warrior (or troll, depending on your chosen side of the argument) on some of his favorite social media groups and message boards.

His first stop today was the GoreWhore message board. It was pretty basic: a black background with ridiculous red font that hurt your eyes after a few hours… a few spinning images that had glitchy transparency that suggested you donate to keep the board alive. No one used message boards anymore, but this one was still kicking. Every day, a dozen or so posts would appear with photos of true crime or leaked accident photos. Videos of graphic collisions, suicides, shocking extreme sports gone wrong. Some of it was a little more innocent than that: fake snuff films and low-budget exploitation films. B-films lived another life on GoreWhore. Here they were blockbusters. This was the place for those producers, writers, and directors to reach cult status.

It was a guilty pleasure. Some people like foot porn; some people like gore and splatter films.

Last night he had harassed this asshole with the screen name 'rainyday666.' Rainyday was a douchebag who thought he was the most extreme person on the forum, constantly suggesting that he *might* have this alternative life where he *might* have some experience doing things that *might* be illegal. Oh, how everyone would regret it if they met him in real life. He would make them regret it. Noah scoffed at the thought, and finally told him off. He didn't just put him in his place; he publicly humiliated him, much to the delight of half of the board's regulars.

He sipped his cooling coffee through his straw, snorting quietly at the notification list of people giving him their support and jumping in the fight against Rainyday.

Noah laughed again, scrolling through and giving a thumbs up to each and every comment, whispering, "Yeah, see that. Nobody likes an edgelord. Suck my dick, rainyday666."

That was when he noticed an instant message. He sat down his cup, squinting behind his glasses as he leaned forward. The message was from someone with the screen name 'vixxn'. She had been a member of the board for four years, and her profile picture was of a busty, pale girl with black hair and dark eyeliner. She was holding a skull a la Shakespeare, pouty lipped and staring into its (lack of) eyes.

Noah would admit he had been suckered by more than one set of tits driven by some random dude in India vying for his credit card number... but here he was, responding with a hard on.

VIXXN: HES SUCH A DICK. IM GLAD U TOLD HIM OFF

NOZARK: THANK YOU. IT WAS OVERDUE.

VIXXN: WANT TO GET HIM BACK EVEN MORE ???

NOZARK: WHAT DID YOU HAVE IN MIND?

VIXXN: USERNAME RAINYDAY666 PASSWORD SNUFFBOX2323

NOAH LEANED BACK IN HIS CHAIR, STARING AT THE SCREEN. HE LACED his fingers behind his head, puffing air nervously between his lips. Vixxn's green activity dot turned to grey to signal she'd moved to away. Was this some kind of trap? Prank? He moved his mouse to hover over the LOG OUT button. Instead he went to his desktop, deciding to opt for a more secure browser, one that wouldn't leave so many traces of him and all of the places he visited. Just in case.

He returned to the GoreWhore site, typing in the newfound login information. He almost gasped out loud when the notification *'Please wait, loading your profile'* popped up across the screen.

"Okay, okay," he said, rubbing his sweating palms on the bathrobe across his thighs as he suddenly saw rainyday666's complete profile. First things first, he changed his profile picture to a photo of a cartoon penis because why not? Then he changed his password to something just as flattering, changed his bio to a graphic short story about fucking his own grandmother... and that was when he noticed an unread message in Rainyday's inbox.

He laughed, "Oh, this is too good."

Noah opened the inbox, fully prepared to send some really nasty messages in response to anyone who had carried on a conversation with Rainyday, but that was when he saw the unread message, sent just a few minutes ago, titled RSVP.

He opened the message, and saw it was from an Elite Member called TheDirector. It read: *Mr. Roth. We have received your applications and are pleased to say that you have been approved to attend the next showing at the theatre. Please arrive fifteen minutes early with a change of clothes for everyone in your party. Your payment has been processed successfully for all four members of your party. The address is 467 Grove Place in New Ashton. When you arrive, tell the clerk at the ticket booth that you are there for the matinee.*

Noah jotted down the address and some other pertinent information and deleted the message from both the inbox and the trash.

He did a search on the forum for posts by TheDirector, finding that he did very little posting on his own, but plenty of people posted *about* him, especially in the speculative forum. There was talk of a secret society, and a very realistic, immersive torture experience somewhere at a remote facility. Everyone was dying for an invitation, and rainyday666 recently bragged about him and his pals having a good chance at getting in.

Well, *had* a good chance at getting in.

JACK BRUSHED his teeth furiously when he was distracted, often until his gums were bleeding and pink. The metallic tang mixed with the minty flavor of his toothpaste, and he spat without looking, nearly missing the sink but salvaging his clean and pressed t-shirt featuring some 80's grindhouse flick.

He had zoomed in on a picture of a woman, presumably dead on the asphalt of a road. She'd ripped off her clothes on the pavement, pieces still stuck to the concrete, and her body was contorted and mangled to the point of looking fake.

He minimized the photo and returned to the group chat.

JACK: SICK!

Phil: car accident this am. ejected from vehicle. wear your seatbelts, boys!

Jack: I got a copy of a banned korean torture film whenever you guys have time to watch it. I read that it makes American Guinea Pig look like birthday party footage.

Noah: I got something to top everything.

Phil is typing...

. . .

BEFORE HE COULD SEE PHIL'S RESPONSE, JACK'S DAUGHTER RUSHED through the door screaming, nearly knocking him over as he clung to the vanity to gain his balance.

"Hey, hey. Slow down and stop screaming. Are you ready for school?" Jack said, spinning around to catch her mid-stride.

She squealed, grinning at him with her missing teeth.

"You got something on your mouth, Daddy," she said, snickering.

"I do?" He looked over his shoulder at the mirror, where he noticed he had copious amounts of toothpaste froth still around his lips.

"Oh, no... Oh, no..." he said, eyes wide. "I'm becoming one of them. One of the undead!"

He snarled at her and she screamed, giggling and kicking. He set her on the ground, and she took off running into the kitchen.

He peeked back down at his phone, seeing that he'd missed a string of messages between Phil and Noah, no doubt arguing about who had contributed the most shocking content to their relationship.

The three men had been best friends since college, brought together over their mutual obsession with the extreme and the macabre. It was hard to top Phil's stuff. Ever since he had started working as an EMT, he would sneak photos to them whenever possible. Highly illegal, highly immoral, highly disrespectful, but *highly satisfying.*

Noah could be a real dick sometimes, always looking to one-up everyone else. He didn't mean anything by it, though; both Jack and Phil knew that. He was one of the nicest and most generous people Jack had ever met, but it didn't take away from the fact that he could be really annoying sometimes.

Jack himself was the quietest one, he supposed. Sometimes he felt like he was just... there. He just bought nasty movies on online auctions and hosted movie nights in his basement with stovetop popcorn and vodka. They often joked that he was the housewife, asking him if he'd wear an apron and make them muffins. He kept his clothes clean and pressed, hair trimmed neatly, face clean shaven. Noah looked like he was homeless half the time, and Phil was doomed to become the classic barbeque dad with a beer gut if he kept it up.

Jack's wife was stuffing food into a lunchbox on the island as he walked blindly into the kitchen. "I need you to drop off two packages to the post office on Saturday morning."

He retrieved a jug of orange juice, sniffing it out of habit before pouring a pulpy glass. "Why can't you do it on your way into town? Won't you be going to pick up groceries?"

"Jack, this is the weekend me and the kids are going to Mom's. Remember?"

"Right. Yeah, I forgot about that."

"The packages are in the office."

Jack had zoned out, sipping his orange juice as he sent a message to the group to let them know he had the house for the weekend. He asked Noah if he could get some weed. Neither one of the guys was paying attention to him; instead, they were arguing about the most gnarly films they'd shared this year.

"...Saturday before noon, they close at noon. Jack? Are you listening to me?"

Jack laid his phone down on the counter, looking up at her. "What? Yeah. I got you. Saturday before noon, packages from your office."

She looked at him dubiously, brow pulled down over her brown eyes. Her lower lip pouted just a little bit. He smiled at her apologetically, looking down quickly enough to see Noah's message: *Jack's wife is out of town, so let's do it.*

PHIL HADN'T HAD time to change his work clothes, so he was dressed in black cargo pants and a maroon top that proclaimed PHIL ILES - HERESY COUNTY EMS - CCEMT across the breast. He crossed the street, waving his hand at a couple of people who waved at him first. He didn't know them, and he kind of figured they didn't know him either. If you were dressed in an emergency services uniform, everyone knew you.

Phil didn't mind this small town celebrity status. If he was being honest, he actually enjoyed the attention. If he wasn't wearing his uniform, he was usually wearing a t-shirt that let you know he worked in emergency services. Phil would argue that it was cooler than being a cop.

He walked through the door of the cafe, seeing that Noah and Jack were already seated across from each other in a booth. He smiled and approached, glad Jack was sitting closest to him. It was a good excuse to choose to sit by him instead of Noah.

As he sat down, Noah slid his soda over to him. Diet Coke, which was what he always ordered. What a joke. He had never successfully dieted a day in his life, but the habit of ordering a diet soda so he could claim he was trying stuck.

Jack drummed his fingers on the table, leaning across the table to speak quietly to Noah, "So you said you had something crazy?"

Phil quietly sipped his Coke, brows raised. "Better than that shit you ripped off of Gore Core, I hope. I've seen better effects at my daughter's school plays."

Noah's cheeks reddened just a little bit. "Yeah, yeah... Don't we enjoy B films, too? We had some good laughs, didn't we?"

Jack encouraged him, hating the banter between Noah and Phil sometimes. He couldn't stifle the sympathetic embarrassment. "I know. Sometimes you just want the next best thing, though. You know? It's hard to top what we've already seen."

Noah scoffed, ripping the paper off of his own straw. "Well, yeah it's hard to top Phil sending us actual accident photos of real dead people."

Phil patted the air as though to have him lower his voice as he spoke, and Noah obeyed, then said, "Alright... I think I've got it. The thing. The next big thing."

Jack waved his right hand in a spiral at the wrist. "Well, come on, spill it. What is it?"

"So, apparently there's this exclusive theater in this town called New Ashton. Couple of hours away, near Rotten Fork. It used to be an opera house type setup, I think. Now it's this club."

Phil cleared his throat. "And?"

"Rumor has it they set up this immersive experience. From what I understand it looks and feels really real. Like *participating* in snuff."

Noah's eyes were lit up, corners of his lips pulled into a broad smile. Jack ran his tongue across his own teeth, reminding himself that he should probably try those whitening strips that his wife had bought him. He looked over to exchange a skeptical look with Phil.

"Why haven't we heard about it before?" Jack asked quietly.

"Really exclusive, like I said."

Phil interjected this time, waving the waitress away to give them a few minutes as she briefly stopped by, much to Jack's dismay. "If it's so exclusive, how are we getting in? We're a couple of average Joes who collect horror movies and action figures."

"I got us in. Just have to trust me. I have a friend in the know."

Jack cleared his throat, tucking his arm around his stomach as it growled. "How much is it to get in? I can't spend a ton or Teckla will know, and I can't..."

Phil laughed. "Do we get a safe word?"

Noah put his palms up. "I've got you guys covered, don't worry about it. My treat. Already have us reservations for tomorrow night."

Phil leaned in. "What's our alibi?"

Noah looked puzzled. "What do you mean?"

"Me and Jack are married. We can't go play in some make-believe murder house without an alibi."

Jack looked up at the ceiling to avoid laughing, whispering, "We could tell them we're doing a kinky escape room."

Noah hadn't thought that far ahead. Of course he hadn't forgotten that they were married with families, but sometimes he forgot that you had to *tell* your wife where you were.

"Tell them you're going to the theater. It isn't a lie."

Phil and Jack sat with identical postures: leaned back against the booth with their arms crossed over their chests. Noah knew they'd already made their decisions, but they just didn't want to admit it. That was fine, because Noah was patient.

"Just think about it... and let me know," Noah said, shrugging as he picked seeds out of the lemon in his tea, flicking the slick white ovals onto the table with his straw.

Phil cleared his throat loudly. "Alright. Okay. I'm in. But if we get there and it's a bunch of rednecks fucking a donkey or some shit, I'm going to kill you. New Ashton... Shit doesn't happen in New Ashton."

On cue, Jack nodded more reluctantly. "Yeah. I'm in."

4

I<small>T WAS</small> funny how you could get lost as far out into the country as they found themselves that night. As the sun went down, they were only threatened to become more lost. Nothing good would greet them in the night out here; the three had collectively seen enough movies with hillbillies to know exactly how this ended for them.

Phil was at the wheel of his SUV: it smelled faintly of spoiled milk and baby powder. A booster seat and a massive car seat were crammed against the back window, completely obscuring the view of the road behind them. Phil's wife had insisted on a minivan, but Phil convinced her to compromise. He still had the stick family decals on the back window and toddler snacks ground into the carpet… but at least it wasn't a fucking minivan.

"We need to get some directions," Jack insisted quietly from the backseat. It was no surprise that he was stuck back there. Any time the group of them went anywhere, he was forced into the back, even though Phil often looked for any excuse to not have to sit with Noah… Noah wanted a front and center for everything and always beat Jack to the door.

Phil grumbled, leaning forward as he torqued his hands around the wheel, "We aren't lost yet."

Noah agreed with Jack, for once. "I don't think we want to get to the point where we *are* lost out here, Phil. The GPS doesn't know where the fuck we are. We don't want to be late either. What if they don't let us in if we're late?"

"Fine, fine. Going to a fucking torture simulation with the biggest fucking pussies on the planet."

Jack settled back into the seat, satisfied. Phil pulled off of the desolate road, front tires spinning against the moist ground as he veered back in the opposite direction. There had been a service station just a few miles back, one of the only signs of civilization they had come across since they'd passed out of Heresy County.

It was a tiny place: a concrete block building that was half as wide as the area for the two pumps and had products crammed on every surface that wasn't otherwise occupied by beer coolers. There was an unattached restroom at the back of the parking lot with a flickering yellow light and a door handle that threatened to fail when you turned it. Jack had briefly considered using the bathroom before they got to the theater, but quickly changed his mind. He pushed the door open with the toe of his sneaker, the smell of ammonia hitting him like a solid force. There was a leaking, used condom hanging off of the front of a toilet seat, and the sink was hanging off of the wall, a steady drip falling from the pipes and leaving a stagnant and growing pool of water on the floor. He swore there was algae growing on the walls.

He opted to piss on the outside of the building instead, choosing a dark area that was away from the dying light, wiping his hands on his pants before he headed back into the convenience center.

He held the door open for a woman who was walking out and found that Noah and Phil were just approaching the counter. Phil took the lead, as usual, stepping forward confidently to lean on the counter. There was a plexiglass or plastic barrier hanging between him and the cashier, but it was streaked with filth and looked like it might have been sneezed or spit on more than once from both sides.

"Which pump number?" the cashier asked. He was a sleepy looking young man, tall and slim with prominent eyes that somehow both bulged from and receded into his eye sockets. His hair was thin and dry, sticking out like thick pieces of straw had been glued to his flaking scalp.

"We're just needing some directions, actually," Phil said with a smile.

"You're not going to buy anything?" the man asked, brow furrowing and nose scrunching, effectively pulling up his top lip to reveal graying buck teeth.

Phil's smile faltered, but he laughed. "No, just need some help. Got a little lost out here."

"You gotta buy some gas."

Noah and Phil exchanged a look, and then both glanced back at Jack as though they'd just noticed his arrival.

"It'd be really great if you could just point us in the right direction; we don't really need any gas," Phil insisted.

The man was open-mouth breathing, reaching up slowly to pick at a scab on his arm as he looked at the three friends like they were armed and this was a stand-off.

"Look," Jack said, reaching onto a shelf to grab a candy bar. He laid it on the counter and pulled out his wallet, retrieving his green bank card from within. "I'll buy the candy bar, then would you just give us a hand? It would make our night go so much smoother."

"Minimum card purchase is six dollars and twenty five cents. Five dollars for the purchase and a buck twenty five to cover the fees…"

"Jesus Christ," Noah growled, reaching down to pick up a handful of candy bars and lay them on the counter. "Will that cover it? Ring it up, we don't have all night."

The cashier still seemed nervous, ringing up the candy bars one at a time, slowly, typing the cash price in on the register like the amount would differ with each new bar. Then he struggled with the static in the plastic bags.

"Forget the bag," Noah insisted, pulling out his phone and twirling it around on the counter. "Do you know how to get to this theater in New Ashton?"

He leaned over to look at the phone, keeping distance like he was afraid it would jump up and bite him, then he looked up at the men. "I knew I shouldn't help you all out..."

"What's that?" Phil asked.

"Why are you going there?"

"The theater? We have an invitation," Noah said.

The cashier's brows raised, face suddenly softening as he snorted restrained laughter, snot slowly oozing from his right nostril. "Y'all? Invited?"

They exchanged looks again.

"How do we get to the theater?" Jack asked again.

"It's a club," the cashier said. "It's in the old theater, but it's a club. What do you think you're doing? Watching a movie?"

"Do you know how to get there or not?" Noah said, stepping forward next to Phil, who had at this point given up.

Even with the barrier between them, the shy cashier took a step back. Noah was not the tallest of them, but there was always something intimidating about him. He was broad shouldered and firm browed, with a strong jaw beneath his thick beard. He had always been the one who could act like the tough guy.

"Yeah... you're going to go a few miles east." He pointed, like they may not know which direction that was. "Then you'll come to an intersection with a caution light. Turn left. New Ashton is right down that road. The club... theater, is outside of town, you'll have to drive straight through. You'll see a bar called Courtney's, turn down by it and follow the road to the theater. It's way out there, don't stop until the road ends. You got it? You think you got that?"

The men nodded, leaving the pile of candy bars on the countertop. As they loaded up in the car, Jack noticed the boy staring out of the window, eating one of the candy bars as he waved goodbye.

5

DESPITE THE ANXIETY about driving through the dark and empty countryside, then the equally dead town, they found Courtney's fairly easily. It was an old metal building with a pink neon sign that had several missing bulbs. Noah snickered that he thought it looked more like Cunty's. Phil and Jack were less amused. Phil even murmured that it was technically Cutny's. Jack sat in the middle seat, leaning forward like the third wheel in their dysfunctional relationship.

"I don't know about this," he remarked reluctantly, peering out the front window as the dark road grew more narrow and rough. If they could have seen out the back window, they would've noticed that the lights from the bar had nearly disappeared into the distance entirely.

Phil cleared his throat, "It is kind of out here isn't it? Noah, are you sure this place is legit?"

Noah nodded with enthusiasm, "Yeah, trust me. It'll be a night we won't forget. Everyone talks about this place."

The road curved into one lane at last, taking them through a dark grove of trees before opening up to a small parking lot. There was a man standing outside with a flashlight, and upon their arrival he immediately began walking towards the vehicle.

"What's this?" Phil asked quietly, knuckles going white on the steering wheel.

"Maybe a valet?" Noah said.

The man rapped on the window with his fingers, flashlight waving through the glass.

"Yes, sir? Good afternoon," Phil said with a smile.

"Names?" the man asked without introduction or fanfare.

Noah leaned forward. "Roth, party of three. Had one friend duck out on us. Here for the matinee."

Phil's eyes flicked upwards to exchange a confused and concerned glance with Jack in the rearview. The man nodded, thanking Noah as "Mr. Roth," and asked Phil to park at the end of the building and walk straight to the door.

"Roth?" Phil whispered as though the valet could still hear them.

"Just fake names, you know. I mean, if you're married and renting a hotel for escort service, you don't want me to put the reservation under Iles do you? Just an extra precaution in case somebody asks or is looking."

Phil looked over at Noah suspiciously. He didn't believe him, and he didn't trust him. Well... Phil would trust two people with his life: Noah and Jack. So in the grand scheme of things, life or death, he really thought that they had his back. But when it came to making good decisions, utilizing common sense, and having an ounce of self-preservation, Phil *did not trust Noah.*

"Remember what I said about the donkey," Phil said.

"Yeah, first hee-haw and we're out, I promise," Noah snarked.

"Won't they ask for our IDs?" Jack asked. "I'm sure there's like... an age requirement for something like this."

"Nah, I think they check everything ahead of time," Noah insisted. Which, Jack noted, made *no* sense if he had signed up under the name Roth. How do you confirm someone's identity with a fake identity?

Now he was feeling a little nervous. His gut rumbled, turning liquid. He noticed there were only a handful of cars in the parking lot, and he thought that in the dark he saw several men in black with dogs on leashes walking along the edges of the property. He expected it to be packed, people pouring in and out. He had hoped he would hear some people in the parking lot talking about what a wild experience it was, soothing his inexplicable dread.

After parking, the three men unbuckled their seatbelts in unison, exiting the vehicle and walking to the front door together. A bouncer with a metal detector stood at the entrance, instructing each of them to stand with their legs apart so they could be scanned with the wand and patted down. Once they were clear, they went inside to a small lobby. It was very plain, well lit. The carpet was old and smelled like cigarette smoke and piss. Not a good first impression, but overall it was fairly mundane. The only thing terribly out of the ordinary was the choice in wall decor.

Noah went straight to the ticket booth, where a woman with blue and blonde hair stood waiting on them. She was dressed like a waitress you'd see at a strip joint, standing awkwardly inside the little booth in her high heels. Noah told her they were there for the matinee, and gave her his fake name again. Jack heard all of this, but it became muffled as he walked over to the walls, looking up at the large and sprawling paintings and photos of dead animals. Mostly roadkill, he thought, judging by the asphalt they were lying on. They were all in different states of decay, some with maggots that he swore pulsed if he stared long enough at the image. Above the entrance was a dead bird, reduced to nothing but bones except for his blue and black wings.

"Earth to Jack," Phil called across the lobby, hands cupped around his mouth to amplify the sound. Jack snapped out of it, jogging over to the ticket booth to rejoin them.

"Gotta turn in our cell phones and wallets," Phil explained. Jack fumbled around for his phone, shutting it off before he handed it to the woman across the counter. She thanked them with a smile, putting all three of the devices and their generic leather wallets into a black box, which she locked, and hung the key on the wall behind her. As she reached up, her dress rode up in the back, and Jack noted that she wasn't wearing any underwear.

He felt a pang of guilt in his gut, thinking about how his wife would probably kill him if she knew he was here... and did he even want to be here? This wasn't really the vibe he was hoping the place would have. He didn't know what he was expecting, but this wasn't it.

"Did you bring your change of clothes?" she asked.

"Change of clothes?" Phil laughed.

"Oh, shit," Noah said, putting a palm to his head. "We completely forgot about a change. Can we just sign a waiver or something?"

"Wait, why do we need a change of clothes?" Jack whispered between clenched teeth, eyeing Phil for support.

"It is not a problem," the woman said, looking them up and down before she turned around and grabbed three t-shirts out of bins behind her. "Here. Just change into these in the waiting area, please... and enjoy your experience."

As though on cue, the doors underneath the dead bird painting opened, revealing another woman standing with her hand across the opening.

"This way, gentlemen," she said, smiling.

They followed her inside, entering a room that was more dimly lit, with couches along the walls. Another door had a lock and sliding viewer at the top. From the other side they could hear loud music thumping, and a red light shined beneath the crack at the bottom of the door.

They seated themselves, and she handed them each a menu on a thick, black folder as they changed into their black t-shirts. Across the backs were three large, white X's. Jack thought this was ironic, as it was also the shorthand for the straightedge movement. He'd bought into that back in high school: no alcohol, no drugs, no promiscuous sex... Basically a way to claim he was lame on purpose, friends had commented.

And now here they were.

Noah and Phil changed their shirts casually, even with the

woman watching. She didn't seem particularly interested, but she still watched all the same. Jack wrang his shirt between his hands for several seconds before he turned away from her, facing the wall as he pulled off his shirt and slipped on the tight-fitting black one instead.

The three of them sat down and started reading their menus, exchanging glances as they did. Noah's mouth was forming a perfect O as he laughed and cussed under his breath. Phil's face was red, and he was also laughing, more giddy than anything. Jack didn't smile; he was too nervous to smile.

The menu had three different sections: *Choose Your Victim, Choose Your Activity, Add-Ons.*

"Does everyone need a minute longer to look at the menu?" the woman asked, voice breathy and low.

"Oh, I'm going all out," Noah asked. "I want to torture... a woman... and I want a hallucinogenic cocktail."

Jack elbowed him. "You're not gonna do drugs, are you?"

Noah whispered back through the side of his mouth, looking at the hostess, "I mean, they aren't going to give us *real drugs*, Jack... just have fun with it, man. It's a simulation. It's a game."

The hostess wasn't listening, tapping her long nails against a slender tablet in her arms. "How old for the victim?"

"Uh..." Noah grumbled. "I get to pick? I don't know... 40s? How many you got back there?"

"You just select eighteen plus or under eighteen."

"Oh, ew... Eighteen plus definitely, I don't even want to pretend I'm killing a kid, you know?"

She tapped the screen again. From the hall, another woman entered with a silver tray. She wore a short red dress that barely covered her ass, and she came to sit in Noah's lap. He seemed too surprised to talk or move, open-mouth smiling so widely that Jack thought he could count all of his teeth. Jack scooted away from him as the woman tried to throw one of her bare legs over his own lap. This was becoming more uncomfortable by the minute.

"Open wide," she giggled to Noah, who was already gaping. She stuck what looked like a piece of thin paper to his tongue, and then gave him a drink in a martini glass. He tried to drink it, dribbling it down his beard and chin as he laughed excitedly. She took the olive out of the glass on a toothpick and encouraged him to eat it. Jack thought on second glance that it wasn't an olive at all… but maybe a small piece of dried mushroom.

Phil was looking at the menu like a connoisseur at a high-end wine bar, rubbing his chin, "I think I'll take sexual free-for-all, eighteen plus woman, of course. No add-ons. I'm the DD."

Jack was up. The hostess came over to him, smiling, and Phil and Noah looked at him expectantly. He thought Noah's face was drooping on one side, and maybe one of his pupils was larger than the other one. Maybe that was all in Jack's head. As his anxiety ramped up he wasn't sure.

"I… I don't think I want to do anything. I might just sit here, wait on you guys?"

"Ah, come *on*, Jack," Phil said. "It's just for fun. We never get out and have any *fun* anymore. Come on. Nobody's gonna know."

"Don't be a pussay," Noah slurred.

Jack swallowed back his nervousness and fear. "Okay. Just surprise me."

The waitress smiled and scrunched up her nose like a child had shown her some of their terrible macaroni art and she was having to act supportive. "I've got just the thing."

6

NOAH HAD DONE plenty of drugs in college. He loved to have a good time, as long as nobody was getting hurt, so he rarely turned down an innocent offer of recreational substances. He never hit anything hard: no heroin, meth, cocaine, prescription pills... but he'd smoked a ton of weed, licked a few blotters, and eaten a few shrooms. That kind of thing. Other than making the mistake of watching classic cartoons when he was high on shrooms, and underestimating a batch of edibles... it had been mostly fun.

He was not prepared when he started feeling the effects of the very real psychedelics of his cocktail. The hostess had opened the door and led them down a hallway with red lights and black wallpaper. It hurt his head. He saw blue and green traces of the woman in front of him as she stopped at a room and let him inside. He put his palm out to the wall to steady himself, and he felt like it was becoming part of his hand. When he pulled his hand away, his fingers felt large and warped. When he looked at them, they were as large as sausages with bulging veins and oozing fingernails.

Dicks. It looked like he had dicks for fingers.

"What was it?" he asked, tongue also feeling like it was outgrowing his mouth. He struggled to keep it inside his lips, feeling it lap around his chin as the woman ushered him into the door. He had serious cottonmouth, and panic crept up as he felt like he couldn't swallow. He talked himself through it. It was okay. Just cottonmouth.

"What's that?" she whispered through the door, voice barely audible under the sound of the music thudding in the hallway behind her. She leaned against the door, facing him like she was trying to be seductive. Noah would've fallen for it too, had she not been morphing into a sexy version of Edvard Munch's *The Scream* right before his very eyes.

"The drink," Noah whispered back. Why was he whispering too? He cleared his throat, speaking louder but no less slurred.

She laughed quietly, reaching out to trace her fingers across his chest. Her touch sent hot, electric waves throughout his entire body, and he shivered as she answered, "A little acid, a drizzle of psilocybin, a dash of mescaline, all mixed in a delicious blend of ayahuasca and just a little grenadine for flavor."

"Oh, grenadine," Noah smiled at the innocent thing. Cherry flavor. He used to order a cherry Coke made with grenadine any time he was at a restaurant with a bar.

"Enjoy your experience, Mr. Roth," she said with a smile, shutting the door against his nose.

Noah leaned against the closed door, hair standing on end. He could hear something moving behind him, and when he turned, he saw someone huddled in the far corner. The room was dimly lit but very clean... not that Noah noticed the hygiene of the place. He knew he had requested a woman, he could remember that much, but that thing in the corner had turned into a creature. Like an alien. One of the grey ones with the eyes that pulled and sagged down like the rogue yolk of a sunny-side up.

She made a noise, a single syllable that he tasted instead of heard. The flavor of the word rolled across his tongue, jaws tingling as he went from being dry-mouthed to producing far too much saliva. It took him several seconds, which felt like hours, to wade through the taste of the word and decipher what its crisp, iron-rich tang meant.

"Help…" the alien squeaked again, voice both guttural and shrill.

Noah opened his mouth, a sudden surge of empathy causing tears to pour from his eyes. A thick rope of saliva poured from the now puckered edges of his lips.

"What?" he sobbed. "How can I help you?"

"Get me out of here," it said; it begged.

Too many words with too many flavors. Noah was going to be sick to his stomach. He vomited, microwaved calzone coming up almost intact, a reminder that he had to stop literally wolfing down food, before a series of mashed junk food followed. With the expulsion, he suddenly realized that he regained a sense of smell. The odor of both his own vomitus and the excrement of the alien assaulted him, causing another wave of nausea.

The room kaleidoscoped into fragments of rust and blue before their jagged edges came together seamlessly, only quivering lightly at the cracks to reveal a reality that was somehow even more terrifying than the drug-induced stupor that was threatening to return.

The room was mostly dark, except for a dull, yellow light in the corner that illuminated a naked woman. She was on the floor on her knees, leather straps causing her breasts and small pockets of fat to bulge over and under. She had a ball gag in her mouth, but she had managed to dislodge it enough to speak… at no small cost. There was blood pouring from her mouth and a piece of broken tooth on her chin, which looked to have been rubbed raw on the floor or wall.

"Please, help me," she whispered. "You don't have to do any of this. Please."

Noah was still steep in his delirium, and he noticed for the first time that what had been her alien eyes were actually bloody craters where her human-eyes had once sat. They looked crisply burned, like the crust on a good brisket, fresh blood peeking beneath the flaking, scabbed edges.

"Oh, god…" he whispered. "This isn't real… This is just a game… just a simulation. Pull it together. Pull it together…"

"Please…" she croaked at him again.

Noah had this strange feeling that there was something too real about all of this. He had been so excited to participate, but now that he was here... he didn't think he had it in him. Not only that, but why did he feel like he was actually tripping?

He tried to get up and turn away from the woman with no eyes, stumbling away as his feet started to feel like they were melting into the floor like spent wax. He stumbled into a mobile counter: a little metal thing that clattered when his body collided with it, scattering a series of items across the floor.

Noah fell onto the ground beside them, face going numb as it too began to feel like it was turning to liquid. The sensation made his scalp itch, and he thought he could hear the skittering call of cicadas somewhere in his head. On the floor with him were various knives and other sharp tools. With a shaky hand, he reached out and grabbed one of the knives, holding it up in the dim light. It glinted brightly, and he could tell it was sharp... *actually* sharp.

"Shit... shit, shit. I'm coming," Noah called to the woman, who was slowly transforming back into the naked, grey-skinned alien... *but at least she had eyes.*

He crawled over to her, reaching out to gently pat her on the arm. She screamed, jerking away from him. He tried to gently quieten her, reaching back to cut the straps that were tied around her ankles, then the strap on her wrists. She fought against him now that her legs were free, and in the struggle, Noah sliced off her pinky finger.

He thought at first that he had just nicked her with the blade; his vision was still playing tricks on him, fighting against the taste of sounds and words, and the fracturing visual reality around him. Not until he saw it fall to the floor, and blood started pouring from the nub, did he realize that he'd amputated the entire thing. It had happened so easily, the sharp blade cutting through it like it was paper. The loose pinky crawled across the floor like a plump maggot, disappearing into the recesses of the darkness.

She screamed. His mouth was full of marbles at the sound: a hard mass of little glass balls that clinked painfully against his teeth and tasted cold and bland. He struggled against them to speak to her, to apologize, tears and snot running down his face. She fumbled around, knocking the knife out of his hand with her wrist. She heard the blade clatter to the floor, and she was on top of it before Noah even realized that he was still perceived to be the enemy here.

She had the knife in her hand, swinging wildly with feral snarls as she lunged in his direction. Noah didn't have the grasp on common sense to realize he needed to be quiet. Instead he apologized loudly, directing the blind girl to where he stood.

She jabbed at him this time, the tip of the knife coming dangerously close to Noah's gut. He instinctively reached down to block her, blade slicing through the flesh of his palm. He screamed, spinning away from the woman as he clutched his injured hand by the wrist. A gaping crevasse formed across his hand, creating two floppy lips that screamed for him, spitting blood. The woman had fallen to her knees, sobbing.

Noah ran to the door, trying to be quiet, trying not to remind her that he was there and he was alive. He struggled with the doorknob, coating it with the sticky, wet blood from his wounded hand as he tried to turn it. The knob was fighting against him, it seemed, and he felt the room shifting around him again. He begged his brain to fight for a sliver of sanity for just a minute. He had to get out of here. He used the bottom of his shirt to try and get traction on the door handle as he felt like he was being lifted up out of his body, physical form feeling heavy and cumbersome.

Then he heard Jack screaming somewhere in the building.

7

PHIL HAD to hand it to Noah: this was pretty fucking sick. The entire place had a very realistic underground air, and the 'menu' for their experiences were wild. He had noted the cost for each thing on the side and thought surely those prices were fake. Noah didn't have a lot of money; he literally sold action figures online that he found at second-hand stores and garage sales. He never held down a steady job. The little picturesque house with the picket fence that he lived in was his mother's. When she died, she left it to Noah, who was her only son. Phil really didn't know how he afforded to keep the lights on.

He was a little nervous for Jack. Although Jack was actually the oldest of the trio by at least six months, Phil had always felt a little fatherly and protective over him. He'd never admit that, but he was inclined to take the vulnerable under his wing, and Jack was definitely the most vulnerable. Phil hated that he was reluctant and scared, but he thought he would have a good time once he got inside. When the realistic facade faded and he realized it was fun, just a game, he could relax. Wasn't this kind of a thing a dream for people like them? They always sat on the couch, screaming to the people on television what they should do in these situations. Now they were going to get to play the game.

The woman ahead of them spoke very robotically. Phil noted that there was what seemed to be a purposeful lack of an accent. "When you are done with your individual experiences, the show is available. It will last approximately thirty minutes. It looks like Mr. Roth did secure you all seats. We will review the etiquette for the theater presentation when you're done. Just come to the end of this hallway, and we will direct you to the theater."

"Thank you, we're very excited," Phil said.

After Noah was dropped off in his dark room, Phil was taken to his own. Jack hung back quietly, but before Phil was even allowed inside, a second woman had come and taken him by the arm, leading him even farther down the red hall.

Phil's escort opened the door, bowing to him low enough that he was afraid she was going to pop a tit over the topline of her dress. Phil smiled at her and slipped inside. She shut the door behind him as she wished him an enjoyable encounter.

The room smelled strangely clean. Not the odor he expected. The floor was black tile marbled with gold. It left a gentle shimmer under his feet in the subtle light. He took a step forward, hesitant, to a workbench on his left. All sorts of sex toys lay across the surface. Phil laughed quietly, wishing the guys were there to gawk at everything with him. Dildos of all sizes, whips, clamps, a funnel and tube, and a few bottles of lube and…

"Sulfuric acid?" Phil read the label aloud to himself. Surely that was some kind of joke… part of the role play. Before he could consider it much longer, he heard a click, and a light came on in the center of the room.

There was a woman there, standing bent over with her stomach resting on a table, each leg strapped apart. Phil wasn't sure how, even in the dark, he hadn't noticed her before. She was completely naked, which caught Phil off guard more than anything. He was a married man, and had four kids. He watched porn regularly, even some of the sketchy shit, but this was something completely different. He caught himself backing away from the girl until he bumped against the work desk and caused it to make a sound. She flinched, raising her head as though she was groggy. She groaned, body tensing as she pulled against her restraints.

When he chose this he thought it would be more like a strip-tease, otherwise it would be illegal. He thought he might be a little nervous, sure, but he told himself he wouldn't feel guilty. Even if things got a little out of hand, he had been looking for an excuse since his wife had cheated on him with that dorky kid from accounting. Jack had always told him he'd regret cheating on her, and that it wouldn't fix anything... but Phil figured he'd rather find out. Unfortunately, he didn't want to pursue anyone, didn't want to make an emotional connection; that would be going too far. So he assumed that when he got this chance he'd be nervous... probably blow his load in his pants halfway through the lap dance, but this was different.

Phil was terrified. *Absolutely horrified* by the presentation of ivory and pink flesh, the vulnerability, the way that it somehow felt non-consensual. He knew that's what they were paying for, but for some reason even when he knew it was fake it just didn't hit him right.

He wandered over to the girl, leaning down near her face. She looked up at him, eyes half closed. She acted like she had been drugged, smiling at him and trying to speak, a small amount of saliva dribbling from her lips. She had fresh purple bruises and spider-webs of red that extended from her eyebrow. There was a pile of vomit on the floor, and the crust on her lips suggested that it might have been hers.

Just... a game.

"Hello?" Phil said, looking into the corners of the room for a camera of some kind. The girl was making noises now, soft mewling sounds. She arched her back and writhed against the restraints. Her pupils were blown out, when he could see them. Her eyes rolled so much that he barely got a glimpse of them. She reminded him of numerous people he had picked up who were high on ecstasy or other party drugs. Disco biscuits, his partner used to call them. He used to laugh at that and had even named his fantasy sports league team that one year. Now it didn't seem so funny.

This was probably a set-up of some kind… If he didn't at least play along, follow through, they were going to think he was a coward. He could see it now: they would joke about how he chickened out in the face of a naked girl tied up when that was *exactly* what he'd asked for. But how far were they going to let this go?

He approached behind the girl and cleared his throat, looking back over his shoulder like he was afraid someone might be standing there watching. He touched her bare hip with his hand, her skin erupting with goosebumps as she rolled her body into him as much as she could. She moaned, burying her face into the table beneath her. Definitely *acted* like she'd had X, but that wouldn't happen. Actors, people employed by these places surely had to take drug tests. A place like this, as prestigious as Noah let on that it was, wouldn't be able to get away with having actual drugs.

But the closer he got to the girl, the more she smelled like sex and sweat and musty piss. This wasn't a tidy, sterile game. This wasn't some plastic girl or virtual reality. This was real. Although the red flags were up, alarm bells causing his ears to ring feverishly, he kept telling himself that this was okay. It was legal; it was an establishment. This was something that people paid to do. *They paid for this*. It wasn't real rape or torture. That was a ridiculous concern. It was all fine. Everyone was fine.

In the flickering beam of the light above them, he saw that she was dripping thick strands of viscous fluid from between her legs, it creeped down her quivering thighs as she fought against the table. Phil reached into his pants and was almost repulsed by himself: limp, soft, almost like he was trying to shrink away from the situation at hand. The girl was laughing now and, although he knew that she couldn't look back far enough to see him and that she was giggling in her delirium… it made him even more self-conscious. Now was not the time to have *performance anxiety*. He closed his eyes, muttering to himself.

"Susie works in a shoeshine shop…. Where she shines she sits, and where she sits she shines… Susie works in a shoeshin shop, where she shines she shits, and where she shits she… Fuck…" He repeated the tongue twister slowly over and over, trying to think of something that would help turn him on. If this naked girl sprawled out on a table couldn't, what could?

He hadn't expected this, but he'd shaved his balls for the first time in years all the same. *Just in case*, you know. You don't want to be caught with your pants down and looking unprepared. He took another deep breath, reaching into his back pocket for the single just-in-case condom.

Heart rate finally slowing, sweat beading around his hairline, Phil finally committed to unzipping his pants.

8

JACK WASN'T happy about being split up from the group. His gut was in a bad, bad way. He could feel it gurgling like a clogged drain, and he was sweating. The girl had taken him by the fingertips, holding just those fingers in her entire small hand. She looked back over her shoulder at him several times, smiling shyly. Jack wasn't a betting man, but he'd wager she was anything but timid.

"Couldn't decide?" she asked.

"Ah… I like surprises," Jack lied. He actually hated surprises. Every year he would log onto his wife's email to see what she ordered for Christmas, so he knew how to react appropriately. When he watched a significant movie, he always read about the ending first. Jack didn't *like* to be surprised, and he didn't crave the unknown like some people did. It wasn't exciting for him; it was anxiety-inducing. Like this whole fucking scenario.

"This is your room here," she said, slipping a black key into the lock and turning the knob. They went into the dark room together, and the girl gestured to a leather outfit hanging beside the door.

"This is yours. If you want to go ahead and strip down, I'll help you get everything on."

"I'm supposed to wear it?"

She looked up at him in surprise.

Jack could feel his cheeks reddening, then his ears. He cleared his throat, eyes darting to the door behind her, "I don't want…"

"Oh, if you're worried about your friends seeing you in all of your glory," she snickered. "Don't worry. This room is totally private, unless you want someone else in. This is *your experience.*"

"Right," Jack said quietly. Except it wasn't his experience. He was perfectly content watching shitty movies and eating snacks at home. He didn't need this.

He was too polite to outright decline the woman's help as she motioned to his shirt like an insistent parent, pulling the strappy thing off the wall. He always had trouble saying no. When he got the wrong food in the restaurant, his wife would have to send it back for him, otherwise he would just eat it. Jack was a yes-man. Jack didn't want to hurt anyone's feelings, or disappoint.

He pulled off his shirt, crossing his arms over his pale and slim torso. The woman held up the outfit as though she were seeing if it would fit, and that was when Jack really got a look at what it was made of.

"You mean my … You mean my junk is going to be hanging out?" Jack asked, voice cracking.

The girl blinked at him, looking down at the outfit, and then at his crotch. "Your cock? You don't want your cock out?"

Jack laughed, but it was a nervous noise without any kind of humor to it. He leaned towards her, anxiously whispering, "I mean, I don't need it you know? Like I don't want it just…"

"Ooooh," she cooed, smiling and winking at him. "I understand."

Jack smiled now, a little more authentic. They laughed together briefly, and she pulled down a different outfit. This one was no less revealing, other than the little leather cup that he assumed he'd have to tuck into. The woman looked pleased with herself, and Jack reluctantly offered her a nod and smile.

"Better?"

"Better," Jack responded.

He was nervous about undressing in front of the woman,

turning away from her when he took his pants off. He couldn't believe he was doing this. It was one of those experiences that would probably keep him up at night feeling guilty for weeks. The fact that he didn't want to do this but still went along with it because he felt like he was obligated would bother him even more.

The leather straps went across both shoulders and down his chest, crossing again at his hips. She added leather bracelets and a set of leather anklets.

"These will be your restraint, but don't worry... You have a safeword. Use the safeword and everything stops immediately."

"Really?"

"Yes. You are in total control; you are the customer."

That did make Jack feel a little better, even as his gut twinged when she strapped him in the middle of the room, legs spread apart, arms suspended above his head. His shoulders were already aching and he had just started.

"What's the safeword?" Jack said, trying to raise his voice casually at the end, but he failed to hide his nervous stammer.

"Bluejay," she said.

Jack nodded, and he watched as the girl left the room and was replaced by another woman. This woman was taller, more broad and muscular. She had long, red hair that cascaded over her shoulders and barely covered her breasts. Her nipples sagged just enough that they peeked below the frayed ends of the ruddy curls.

Were people just walking around topless here?

"Hello," Jack said awkwardly.

The woman didn't respond but instead walked over and set down a bag. It was a bulky black thing that he would have normally thought carried a mechanic's tools. She squatted down, resting her buttocks on the heels of her feet as she stirred through, removing something innocent enough: a riding crop.

One end had the traditional leather tongue and the other had a long, artificial, pink feather. The girl stalked over to him, predatory. Jack tensed as she dragged the pink feather down the length of one arm, and then trailed across his chest and stomach, curving around one hip. He twisted away from her, grunting.

"So, what..."

Jack was interrupted by the woman's hand across his face. She slapped him so hard that he saw bursts of grainy red and white stars in his vision, then she backhanded him across the opposite cheek. He heard himself groan involuntarily and he blinked.

"What the fu—"

She flipped the whip over, pressing the rod against his throat as she smirked and wagged a disapproving finger before putting it to her lips to silence him.

"Oh... okay..." Jack whispered, nodding. His eyes were watering, and now his nose was either bleeding or starting to run. The girl returned to the feather, teasing one of his sore cheeks, his neck, and down to the leather cup. He shied away from her again, trying to cross his knees to avoid her touch. He really, really didn't like this.

Even suspended like he was, the woman was tall enough that they could stand eye to eye. She approached him, brushing the tip of her nose against him before she pressed her lips against his. Jack resisted at first, but it was no use. Her tongue grazed against his teeth and hard palate, sloppily forcing his own tongue to the back of his mouth. He thought he was going to gag, maybe even vomit, but she finally pulled away. She seemed disappointed that he hadn't reciprocated her kiss, striking him across the thighs with the leather crop.

He was breathless and sick, reeling from everything that had just happened to him. He couldn't remember the damn word.

"I don't want to do this anymore," he whispered to her, a mixture of his and her saliva pouring down his chin. "I don't know what I'm supposed to say, I don't remember what I'm supposed to say, but I'm telling you I don't want to do this."

The woman still stood there, so close he could smell vanilla and mint on her breath, feel the heat off of her body. She reached up and grabbed one of his small nipples between her thumb and forefinger and squeezed. Jack made a noise in his throat: a pathetic whine.

"Please. I just want to go home. This isn't part of my act or anything. I'm not pretending to be... whatever. I just want to get dressed and get the hell out of this fucking place, *please.*"

She returned to the bag, pulling out what Jack at first thought was a flashlight. Why was the fucking lighting in this room so shitty? Could they not put in a few of those nice LED bulbs? He supposed that would ruin some of the curb appeal. Nobody looked good in the light.

The woman slipped the thing into her mouth, slathering her tongue across the surface and leaving it shining and wet. As she came closer, Jack realized it was a dildo. He belched a sour dollop of bile onto the back of his tongue, swallowing back the burning liquid as he fought for the right word to say to get her to stop. Was she going to fuck herself with that thing in front of him? He clamped his eyes shut briefly, gritting his teeth.

When he opened his eyes back up, however, he did not find the girl sprawled out on the floor, legs splayed, with the massive silicone toy inside her... No, instead, she was walking towards him with that same predacious stare. She had a wolf's eyes: that nearly yellow hazel that glimmered with a raptorial hunger. He thought he could even hear her growl.

"No, what are you doing? Where are you going?" Jack's voice became shrill. When she was behind him, he lurched forward on his restraints, trying to look back over his shoulder at her.

"Fuck, fuck, fuck. Bluebird. Bluebird. *Bluebird.* I said the fucking word. I said the fu—"

He could feel the girl's hand on his left ass cheek, four fingers digging into the side and her thumb reaching between, pinching him so that she could press the tip of the toy against him. It was wet and cold, more flexible and soft than it had looked. He clenched, bouncing against the leather straps again as he screamed in frustration.

"This isn't okay... I didn't say this was okay. This is far enough. I want to get out of here *right fucking now*. I said the fucking word. Did you hear me?"

The woman cooed a word that sounded like 'awww,' clicking her tongue against the roof of her mouth in disapproval, then she plunged the toy inside him.

Jack felt like his body lit up. His gut hurt, his ass hurt, even his fucking balls hurt. He twisted violently, trying to get his wrists loose from the tight cuffs. He felt his right shoulder pop, grinding in its socket as he tried to wrench himself free. He didn't know what he was screaming, but he thought they were words. Maybe pleas for help, maybe 'bluebird.'

She was sliding it back and forth now, each time pressing it so far that Jack wasn't sure where it all went. He briefly wished he could bend over to give it more room, thinking that just maybe it would alleviate the pressure in his bowels. The woman was talking to him now, voice gruff and gravelly. He didn't want to hear what she was saying to him, trying to scream over her. His voice was starting to give out, and instead he started sobbing, wishing he couldn't smell his own shit and hear the sounds of the woman moaning and grinding against him, feverishly rubbing herself as she maneuvered the dildo inside of him.

She briefly reached around him, slathering her sticky and wet fingers across his lips and he was forced to taste the salty-sour flavor of her. He tried to bite her finger, wishing he could snap it off at the bone, but instead her hands moved down and wound around the leather cup, trying to undo the straps holding it on from her position behind.

"Fuck you," he whispered, and started screaming for help again in a hoarse voice.

He thought he could hear someone else screaming and for a moment he took comfort that maybe Noah was also getting fucked in the ass by a redhead.

9

NOAH HAD FINALLY MANAGED to get the door open, leaving the blind woman with the knife inside as he exited into the dark hall. He felt intense empathy, sick to his stomach about her being scared and trapped. He felt guilt about cutting her finger off, about ordering her like she was a fucking filet mignon on a menu.

"What the fuck..." he whispered through tears, over and over, as he made his way down the hall.

He felt himself slipping again. Walking into the hall was walking into a different world. He could barely see: vision pulsing with the dubstep trash that played so loudly that Noah could feel it. His face was numbing on one side, little pins and needles creeping around his lips like a million tiny aphids.

This was the worst trip he had ever had. You didn't mix drugs like this. He remembered the first time he had ever dropped acid. That unassuming piece of paper looked like a colorful stamp and it had made him feel like he was seeing the world for the first time. It was like living was fake, everything before was a dream and being on acid was a glimpse of what was *real*. He had realized so much about the world and about people. The loop had gotten him, that endless roll of actions that seemed to press on forever.

Time dilation was no joke. The hallway was never ending, dripping with rich redness. He thought he could hear his shoes making splashes on the floor, but when he looked down his legs were wisps of black clouds. Like a fucking genie… in the Stanley Hotel.

He turned the knob on one door, shoving it open to see a man and the corpse of a woman. She was dead. One hundred percent, legitimately, certifiably, legally dead. He didn't have to check, because her head wasn't attached to her body anymore. He didn't know where it was, and he didn't care to look for it. He didn't recognize the man standing there in one of the black t-shirts with the three x's across the back, bare ass visible just below the tail of the shirt, body smeared with blood. He was thrusting into the cross section of the woman's neck, balls deep in her trachea.

He stopped when he heard the door open, leaning back to look at Noah. He was panting, smiling. It was a terrible smile: a Cheshire cat grin that split his skull in half, and Noah had to look away to give his mind time to reel itself back in. He stole a glance back at the man, wincing as the corner of the man's mouth still danced with thin tendrils that threatened to exaggerate his grin again. Without the horrible distortion, Noah thought this guy looked like a clean-cut, desk job type. Good looking. Probably could snag women all day (with their heads attached) with a smile and a promise to pay for dinner.

"You wanna come in?" the man asked, motioning to Noah.

"No… No thank you," Noah squeaked, thinking that he could see his voice leave his mouth in dusty pink bubbles.

The guy seemed perplexed, motioning to the body, "You can have the other end and we can get off at the same time."

"That's…" Noah choked. He was afraid he was going to vomit again. *You can shut the door. You don't have to stand here. You can shut the door*, he told himself. His head felt like a bowl that was too full of liquid. He closed the door quickly, walking with his arms out to the side to avoid spilling those imagined contents from his skull as he went to the next door. His quivering hands struggled to turn the knob, but it was secure. So he tried the next.

And the next.

He didn't know how many doors he tried to open before he finally came to another one that was unlocked.

Noah's hand ached painfully as he twisted the door knob, peeking around the corner to see another man and a woman chained to a table.

He tried to be quiet, just in case it was another stranger inside. This one could be less friendly, he told himself. He clutched the door, finding himself disoriented as he peered inside the dark room. Everything was dark other than the man and girl in the center of the room. They were illuminated, glowing. The light hurt Noah's eyes, seeming to pulsate with energy. He felt heavy. He just felt… unwell.

He was both relieved and repulsed when he realized it was Phil inside. There was a girl strapped to the table in front of Phil, who was squeezing handfuls of skin between his fingers as he thrust into her from behind. The girl was moaning but sounded out of her head. Noah thought he could hear her say, "Hey, guy? Hey."

If Phil heard anything, he wasn't reacting.

Noah couldn't repress the nausea anymore and vomited straight through the doorway, spraying hot acid over his tongue and out his nose. It burned and stung and smelled acrid.

"Phil!" he choked, belching as he stumbled inside and slammed the door behind him. "Phil, don't. It's real, it's real, it's real."

By now Noah could feel the tears pouring down his face. It felt good, somehow. A release of tension like a pressure valve had been triggered in his skull. Bile and snot ran out of his nose and the repulsive flavors pooled around his dry lips. He tried to swallow, but his tongue stuck to the roof of his mouth, making a click as he gasped and struggled to breathe.

Phil spun around, leaving a wet streak across the girl's backside. He was covering himself, frantically zipping his pants like he'd try to hide what he was doing. Noah knew though, even through the drugs and delirium.

"What are you doing?" Noah breathed, body wracked with tremors.

Phil rushed over to him, brow concerned. His cheeks were still flushed with embarrassment, the rosy tint riding up his ears and onto his scalp. He pulled Noah into him, squeezing him tight.

"Noah, what the fuck? What is wrong?"

Noah had never met anyone who was as ready to hug you as Phil. It was one of his favorite things about him, although he'd likely never admit that. He breathed in through his nose and out through his mouth as he tried to take the comforting embrace from his friend, but the smell of sex and sweat on him only brought his nausea back. He blew a bubble of snot, which left a stringy mess between his face and Phil's black shirt.

"They drugged me, man," Noah whispered, voice cracking as it rose in pitch. "They drugged me and then there was a girl, and they'd burned out her fucking eyes and I accidentally cut off her finger and..."

Phil pulled away from Noah, staring down at him in confusion.

"Whoa, whoa, whoa. Slow down," he insisted.

"This place isn't right. Everything is real. The girl was hurt and she was scared." Noah jammed his finger in the direction of the woman on the table. "She's real, Phil. You were..."

Noah would have, under different circumstances, chosen his words more wisely. He would have given Phil the benefit of the doubt. Phil was a *good guy*. He was a paramedic. He always did stupid charity events and returned his shopping cart and held the door open for people. He tipped well at the restaurant (so well that Noah had often skimmed the tip when the other guys headed out the door). But Phil had done something really terrible, and Phil was *smart enough to know*.

"You were raping that girl, Phil," Noah said through gritted teeth.

"I wasn't... I..." Phil stammered, voice desperate.

"We've got to find Jack," Noah interjected, closing his eyes. His face hurt; it felt screwed into a painfully sad pose as dramatic and dismayed as Melpomene, that forever dismal muse of tragedy. He caught himself opening his mouth like the iconic mask, clamping his jaw shut when he realized what he was doing.

"Okay, we'll find him."

"I heard him screaming," Noah whispered.

"Do we let her go?" Phil asked, motioning to the girl at the table. He didn't look at her, and Noah figured he probably couldn't.

Noah was torn. He wanted to let her go, because she was a victim. She probably didn't want to be here. Was she kidnapped and trafficked? Seduced? Drugged? On the other hand though, they needed to get out of here. Maybe they could get help once they were outside.

He held up his cut hand and Phil's face drained of color.

"Oh, my fuck, Noah."

Phil grabbed Noah's hand by the wrist, twisting it around towards the dim light to inspect it.

"Can you move your fingers? What happened? This is *really bad*."

"I don't want to move them. They hurt so bad. The girl cut me."

"Why would she do that?"

Noah leaned in, choking out: "Don't you get it, Phil? We're the bad guys."

10

PHIL STEADIED Noah as they went down the dark hallway. If he hadn't been forced to support his friend's struggling form, he would have been sprinting. Now that they had exited his room, he could hear those hoarse cries for help that no doubt were coming from Jack's lungs. Noah sobbed, intensifying with every additional second they had to hear Jack screaming. Phil tried to comfort him quietly, rubbing small circles on his shoulders with his fingertips, cooing in his throat.

He had been so humiliated and surprised when Noah came into the room and caught him in the act. He didn't know why he'd done it. Jesus Fucking Christ. What was he doing? He was almost sick now, confused whether it was guilt or actual regret. He didn't know whether he was sick over being caught, over someone knowing he had chosen to engage when it felt wrong, or if he had truly not known. Had he known? He'd had a bad feeling, but was it because he *knew*?

Was it rape? The girl hadn't consented. Phil had daughters. If she didn't consent, if she didn't explicitly agree, Noah was right. That was the fuel under his twisting gut now. How was he going to live with himself, knowing that he was capable of such a thing?

Noah stumbled against the wall, moaning something about the music as his tongue rolled out of his mouth like a rogue parasite. Phil took the opportunity to side step and free one of his balls from where it had slipped over the seam of his twisted boxers. He felt something wet and heavy slide down his pant leg and he shook his foot like a dog who had stepped in a puddle, letting the condom fall across his shoe and onto the floor. Semen left a snail-trail down his calf, causing the fabric of his pants to stick.

At least Noah was too high to notice the condom that now lay in the hallway.

"This is it," Phil whispered as they approached the door muffling Jack's screams. They had reduced now: half-hearted and more anger than fear. Somehow, Phil was comforted by this. He was still worried that Noah might be suffering some kind of toxicosis. If those drugs were real, he had taken way too much... and who knew what kind of contaminants were in that drink?

They swung the door open, Noah clinging to the door frame as he turned green again around his eyes and mouth.

"Oh, fuck," Phil shrieked.

Jack was suspended with his arms and legs out like a starfish, some twisted crucifixion with leather and chains. He was red faced, sweating. Phil noted a very brief, subtle expression of relief on his face upon seeing the two of them. Phil could swap from villain to hero now, at least for a little while.

He pushed his way inside, dragging Noah along as he shut the door behind them. The odor in the room was pungent, a recognizable scent. A blend of natural affects that meant fear, terror, desperation.

Phil didn't notice the woman behind Jack at first, eyes adjusting from the red of the hallway to the dim, neutral lighting of the room. She peeked around Jack's suspended body and barked.

She truly barked. Her voice was hardly human; it was commanding and feral. The guttural tone was a sort of primitive warning, and Phil caught himself stepping backwards at the sound.

"Hey! You can't be in here," she snarled again, dropping a black dildo to the floor behind Jack. Jack's body instantly relaxed and he let out a long groan of relief, hanging now more placidly in the restraints.

The blood and shit-streaked toy rolled across the floor in a circle before coming to rest on a drain at the lowest point.

"We're just going to go," Phil said quietly, voice calm and attempting to soothe. "Something has come up and we need to take our friend and go. We'll pay a fee or whatever if there is one."

"You can't be in here," she repeated, reaching down into the black bag in front of Jack to retrieve something.

"I know, we're just here for our friend," he insisted calmly.

Phil could barely see what it was with the lack of light, but in his gut he knew it was a gun, even before she swung her arms up, holding the sizable handgun with both hands and her elbows fully extended. The way she clutched the hefty gun awkwardly in her hands suggested she may have never used it before, but she looked so confident that Phil remained glued to the spot.

"Get out."

She had the weapon pointed at Phil, but her eyes darted between him and Noah. Phil had been in these sorts of situations before: at gunpoint, at knife point. He wasn't a total stranger to trying to diffuse. The difference was that the people he was up against were usually hurt or strung out or scared. This woman was in control.

Phil saw Noah squirming as he stood, whining and crying. Noah took a step forward, towards the woman with the gun. He wasn't threatening, but she turned the gun towards him instead. Noah flinched, arms flinging up into the air like he was an innocent guy in a western.

"Do not move unless it is towards the door," she demanded.

Noah started stammering, but he was talking to Jack. Phil couldn't understand him, but he thought he was apologizing. The woman told Noah to back up again, taking one step towards him.

Phil took the opportunity. He wasn't sure where he got the guts, but before he had made a conscious decision to do so, he was tackling the woman. He tucked his shoulder into the deceptively soft curve of her waist and then lifted her off of the ground before he tackled her. The gun flew out of her hand, clattering in the dark somewhere far away. He had half expected her to have fired upon impact, but she was either more controlled than he thought or maybe the gun wasn't even loaded. Maybe it was part of the show, maybe it was a prop. Phil couldn't help but continue to hope this was all just a cleverly organized event.

He had her down onto the ground, grappling for control of her arms as he tried to subdue her. She was brawny and strong, almost as tall as Phil himself and built like a swimmer. She swung a free fist up into his face, and it sent him flying backwards.

She packed a serious punch. Phil saw bright explosions of white and gritty pink and red, ears ringing as the back of his skull collided with the concrete floor.

11

NOAH COULDN'T STAND the sight of Jack hanging in the middle of the room. Everything kept getting worse, which only deepened Noah's incoherence. The woman was hard to lay eyes on. Noah felt like his eyes were rimmed with tears, which made her look scrambled like an old television screen, pixelated and full of writhing static.

He stood with his hands up in the air even after Phil had tackled her to the floor. He was frozen in fear, unsure what he should do to help. Phil struggled with the woman, who was clearly very strong and flexible.

Noah rushed over to Jack, hands shaking as he tried to unfasten his restraints.

"Hurry up, hurry up..." Jack murmured anxiously.

His fingers felt like they were working backwards, every intended movement counterproductive. He stole a glance over his shoulder just in time to see the redheaded woman punch Phil. She didn't just hit him to get away, the punch followed straight through as though she was trying to shove his nose through the back of his skull. Phil fell back, head hitting the floor with a sickening thud.

"Oh, fuck," Noah whispered, waves of prickling pins spreading from his scalp to the soles of his feet. He rolled the back of his head on his shoulders, trying to get rid of the sensation as he successfully freed one of Jack's arms.

"Come on, Noah!" Jack screamed at him.

He'd never heard Jack raise his voice, let alone scream like that. He had to stop and scratch the sensation under his hair, clawing at the flesh with his short nails until clumps of hair were clinging to his fingertips. He heard Jack yell his name again, but that was when something hit him.

All of the air was knocked out of Noah's lungs as the woman took him to the floor. The concrete was tacky like fresh paint, with a fine grit mixed in.

Noah swatted at her, trying to get away. He rolled onto his stomach, fighting for traction until he had broken off two fingernails. They popped off, clinging by frail cuticles, leaving bloody streaks on the floor as he continued to claw away from her.

She pulled him back, hitting him in the side of the face with her elbow. Noah's face felt like it swelled immensely, like a wound in an old cartoon. She straddled his chest and wound her fingers around his throat. He was already struggling to breathe, struggling to swallow. His hands weren't cooperating, movements leaving traces of themselves in front of his eyes so that he couldn't keep up with where his limbs were at all.

The woman scooted forward off of his chest, and he tried to slide out from underneath her, but instead she wrapped her calves around his chest, knees and thighs clamped around his head and neck.

He hadn't been to a gym in ten, fifteen years... The most activity he got was grocery shopping, and he never exercised. Had he known he'd be pinned underneath a dominatrix, breath pushed out of him as she squeezed him with her thighs, maybe he would have tried harder.

Phil was disoriented, Noah could tell by the way he struggled to get to his feet and then how he swayed like something light in the breeze. Like one of those ridiculous inflatables at a car lot. Briefly, through his tears, he thought he could see a shimmer of that frantic flopping in Phil's own body.

Noah slammed closed fists into her legs, watching as Phil reached down and picked something up out of the woman's bag. He got one gasping breath, smelling and tasting the scent that clung to her: like sushi and soy sauce, it made him simultaneously hungry and sick.

Phil was there now, looming behind them. The woman noticed him just a moment too late. When she looked up Phil swung the thing in his hands down, hitting her so hard between the eyes that her head bounced against the floor and back up again. She groggily raised her chin, blood pouring from her nose, bridge swelling tremendously. In the silence between them Noah heard a vibrating sound, like a phone across a table. The object in Phil's hands rose to the light: a thick, rigid purple vibrator with a sizable knot halfway down the shaft. It was illuminated with a halo in the dim luminance like some holy object as Phil held it in the air.

Phil hit the woman again, this time with a swing like a bat. Despite the way her body suddenly felt heavy on top of him, she still snarled and tried to retaliate. She fell over on top of Noah, somehow squeezing him even harder as her body convulsed, spraying hot and musty urine onto his face. It ran into his eyes and up his nose, trickling down to soak his shirt collar.

He dug his fingernails into the fat of her leg, pulling it away just enough to see Phil pummeling her face with the end of the vibrator. She wasn't fighting anymore, although her body reacted to each blow, flinching, tensing muscles quivering.

"Phil," Noah managed to squeak. "Please stop, please stop."

He did stop. He was breathing so hard that during each inhale Noah could see the space between his ribs. His shirt was sweat-soaked and clinging to him, receding hairline dripping with perspiration. His hands and chin were covered in a spray of blood: the faintest and sparsest smattering of cerise droplets. He dropped the vibrator to the floor, still humming, and then he was prying the woman off Noah, saving him from the vice grip of her legs.

Noah rolled over, heaving onto the floor, but he had nothing left to void. He tried to not look at the woman, but it was like his mind was telling him he had to. He had no choice. Her face was a bulbous mess, swelling before his very eyes. The interference in his vision, like images burned into a television screen, made it look like she was moving just a little. He almost thought he could see her breathe, see her lips move to form quiet words. Her teeth were pried out of her gums, roots jutting through her gingiva like insects burrowing up from fleshy soil. What he had initially thought was a piece of her cheek, he realized was part of her severed tongue. At some point she had bitten the thick cord of muscle in half.

Jack had managed to use his free hand to release himself and was on the floor on his knees by Noah in an instant.

The woman suddenly started gasping, chest fluttering up and down, moaning and taking great, heaving breaths. Noah jumped away, pushing himself back.

"Phil?"

"She's agonal," Phil explained quietly. His hands pressed underneath the woman's chin, then her wrist, above her left breast, as he felt for any signs of a pulse or heartbeat. He started giving her chest compressions. It didn't feel like, as Noah watched, that he tried very hard. With every compression she gurgled, bubbling blood spewing from her nose and mouth. He stopped the forceful compressions as soon as the gasping breaths stopped. The woman was very still, and Phil felt her wrist again with his eyes closed.

"What the fuck, you guys?" Jack whispered. "What the fuck?"

"What is it?" Noah asked quietly.

Phil looked over at them, and he shook his head.

"She's..." Jack started hesitantly.

"Yeah, she's dead."

"Oh, no, no, no..." Noah said, sitting up so quickly that his head spun.

"What do you mean, 'no, no, no'?" Jack snapped. "She was shoving a fucking ten inch dildo up my ass. She tried to kill you. She tried to kill Phil."

"She was breathing. She was trying to breathe," Noah insisted. "What happened?"

"It was agonal breathing, Noah. She was already gone. It was her body's last-ditch effort to survive."

Noah didn't protest, but he couldn't stop the tears. Phil had fallen back onto his backside, knees drawn up as he wiped a bloody hand across his open mouth. He muttered quietly, "I fucking killed her..."

"You did what you had to do," Jack insisted, crawling over to Phil. "How's your head, you okay?"

Jack clutched his own gut. Noah noticed for the first time that blood streaked the backs of his thighs. He was mostly naked. Jack didn't even like wearing shorts in public; he hated his chicken legs. Noah was humiliated for him, for his exposure, his violation.

"I probably have a concussion, you've probably got a fucking ruptured colon, Noah's overdosed on god-knows what."

"I am so sorry," Noah said. He didn't know what else to say. He needed to apologize for this. It was his idea. His plan.

"How are we going to get out of here?" Phil asked. "I don't think walking out the front door is an option."

Jack turned to Noah. "Noah, I need you to tell us everything. Where you heard about this place, who knows we are here... everything."

"And why you're using a fake name," Phil interjected.

Noah took a deep breath. "I was on a message board and there's this guy and he's a dick and he just... he went too far talking about one of these indie filmmakers. Just tearing them apart because he could. So I told him off and everyone was into it, you know? They were glad I did it. This girl named... I don't know. Her username was 'vixen' or something. She gave me the guy's login and when I got into his inbox he had an invitation here..."

He watched as Phil and Jack exchanged glances. He swallowed back embarrassment. They were disappointed in him, as always. He was a joke, wasn't he? It's why Phil always had an excuse as to why he didn't invite him to the events the EMS put on, and why Jack's kids called Phil 'Uncle' but not Noah. His gut wrenched in self-pity.

"He had gotten an invite for himself and three friends, so I took the info and deleted the message... I thought it was just a game. A fake experience. I had no idea."

In the silence he repeated that he had no idea, over and over. Phil reached over, unsteady, and put a hand on his urine-saturated shoulder.

"It's alright," he whispered. "We're going to get out of here."

"*How?*" Jack asked.

"I have to get out of here," Noah insisted, stomach tying itself into tight knots that ached and bubbled. "I have a cat at home and I didn't feed him enough before I left. Even if he gets into my cabinets somehow, he doesn't have enough food. He's this cat that just kind of adopted me, and no one has ever wanted me like that cat does. He's this ugly red thing and... I think he's actually someone else's cat because he had on a collar but it only says his name on it and he's so skinny. He loves food and..."

Phil was ignoring everything he said, talking over him to Jack even as Noah's voice trailed off into shunned silence. "The only option we have is to play along. There's some kind of theater thing coming up. A show. We can go, and then when the show is over we'll head out an exit door."

"You really think, after what we've already been through, that it'll be that easy?" Jack was quiet, voice low.

"We didn't know what we were walking into. We were caught off guard. Now we know. We need to play it cool, and get the fuck out as soon as we can."

"What about her?" Noah asked, pointing at the woman. "She's one of them, isn't she?"

Phil shrugged, "I have no idea..."

"This place used to be an actual theater. There have to be fire exits in the main areas. If we can just get outside and get to the car..." Jack said, voice hopeful. "They think we're one of them."

"Right now, yeah," Phil agreed. "As long as they think we're one of them, we should be okay. Safe. What about you, Noah? Can you hold it together? How are you feeling?"

How was he feeling? Noah felt so detached from himself, so separate from his identity and body, that he didn't really know how to respond. He should be coming down by now. Hadn't it been hours? Realistically, somehow he doubted it. Although it felt like forever, he bet they couldn't have been there long at all. All he needed was four hours, six hours... That's all he needed. He'd start coming down. He just had to hang in there and keep it together.

"Getting better," Noah said quietly.

"Alright," Phil said, standing up. "Jack, let's get you dressed... Let's get her rolled over into a corner out of the light. Then we'll go down the hall, meet the hostess, and go to the show."

Jack hesitantly reached between his legs with a shaking hand, pulling it back into the light to reveal his middle finger caked in clotted blood. Noah tried to act like he didn't see him, like he wasn't looking directly at him when he'd dipped the finger into his torn and slack anus.

"Are you okay, Jack?" Noah whispered, and he could feel the tears creeping up on him again like sand in his throat.

Jack swallowed, wiping the gelatinous blood on his calf. "Yeah... I'm alright."

12

JACK WAS HAVING trouble sorting through his emotions in the aftermath of his room experience. He hurt all over, like he was a shirt turned inside out and left wet and cold on a clothesline. He couldn't decide where the pain started and ended, and every step down the hall sent a shockwave through him.

His gut wrenched, tying itself into knots, and he felt himself leaking fluid into his pants. He smelled like shit. Literal shit. He imagined climbing into a hot shower, pressing his body against the cool, clean wall while the heat cleansed him. He lusted after a soft bed with white sheets and a pillow that he'd been breaking in since college, a perfect indention for his head in the center. Like he was sliding into a manufacturer's box where he belonged and fit just perfectly.

Phil was leading them, of course. It was always Phil. Jack was comforted by the fact that he seemed like he wasn't afraid, like he was determined to get them out at all costs. There was something about knowing someone was willing to do *anything* for you in a situation like this. If anyone could come up with a plan and make sure it was followed through, it would be Phil. He was smart and creative and dedicated and brave. He never showed any kind of fear.

Not to them. Jack wondered what had happened in Phil's room, and if he was afraid of what might happen to them if they couldn't get out of here.

He was surprised at how the death of the woman didn't bother him. *His rapist.* If anything, he had felt this sick satisfaction as he watched Phil beat her to death in front of him. He still had sore indentions where his dick had gone rigid inside the leather cup at the sight of her mangled face. He felt a little guilty over the involuntary reaction. He struggled to get a hard on if the lights were on, if he had his mind on something else, if he was embarrassed, if he had a bad day, if his wife tried to talk dirty to him, if he could hear the kids walking around in the hallway... but there he had been, hanging by his arms, mostly naked, in front of his two oldest friends, hard as collegiate arithmetic while he looked down at a woman whose face resembled a charcuterie spread more than a human anymore.

Phil stumbled beside him and brought him back to the present. Jack set his jaw, glaring at the back of Noah's balding head. This was all his fault. He knew that he didn't mean to, rationally he knew that. He knew that Noah would never get them into a situation like this on purpose... but it was still all his fucking fault. Noah never took responsibility for anything, and this would be no different. They always had his back to make sure he never had to experience any backlash for his bad decisions.

The hall curved to the left, and then Jack saw the hostess from earlier standing there as though she had been waiting the whole time. He felt a sinking sensation in his gut as he saw her: smiling, cool and collected. He thought to himself, with as much humor as he could muster, *She's seen some shit.*

She didn't even react to the smell of them as they came within speaking distance. Her nostrils didn't flare, she didn't swallow, she didn't blink. She just smiled.

"Gentlemen, I hope your experiences were everything you hoped for and more. The party is about to start. Please follow me."

The three men exchanged nervous glances but followed the

woman dutifully. She guided them towards a huge auditorium that was filled with people. Jack was shell-shocked. How many people could possibly be involved in something like this? How many of them were there intentionally? By invitation, by payment?

The room was a sea of people with black shirts and x's across the back, and they were all wearing the masquerade style masks. The hostess brought them to a small room where she removed three masks and handed one to each of them. Phil was handed a black wolf, Noah a bronze cat, and Jack...

He took the blue mask with the small black beak into his hands, staring down at it. He had never felt such an anger before, a fury. He would have never thought of himself as capable of such a dark cloud.

"Did you know that bluejays are corvids? Like they're in the same family as ravens?" Noah whispered, already donning his own mask.

Jack looked over at him, eyes venomous.

"You look at a crow and you think, that's creepy or that's bad ass or something. Nobody thinks that about the bluejay, but they're smart and resourceful and *they will fuck you up.*"

"Shut the fuck up, Noah," Jack snapped, putting the mask on.

Wolf Phil stared at the two of them, green eyes glistening behind the mask as he silently demanded they pull it together. Jack closed his mouth, pursing his lips together obediently.

The woman allowed them to go into the auditorium unsupervised, seeming to expect that they would know where they were going and what to do. Phil led them past several couples as they awkwardly tried to mingle with the crowd. The people were too casual, too relaxed for all of the shit the three of them had just been through. Jack surmised that they were probably old pros, people who came here knowing what they were signing up for.

He also knew that nothing that was going to happen in this room was going to be good. No show that this company put on was going to be something they wanted to see. Would it be interactive?

A pang of nausea surged through him. The stage loomed ahead, lights already poised to center stage.

Jack didn't know if he could stomach it. He knew someone was going to die. Not like his grandfather in the nursing home, surrounded by clocks and machines and sterility, pumped full of quiet drugs. Not like someone who had resigned themself to death, accepted it, willed it. People that died here died in a course of chaos; they did not fade but were snuffed out.

There were maybe thirty other people in the room. Jack did a quick headcount out of sheer curiosity and nervousness. Sometimes counting things soothed him: *find five things you can see, four things you can touch, three things you can hear, two things you can smell, one thing you can taste...* But somehow knowing that there were so many nutjobs who enjoyed this type of thing did not offer any comfort.

He was surprised to see a few women in the crowd as well, wrists tucked against their breasts as they cradled glasses of wine. A bar lined one wall, with an attentive bartender in a fox mask waiting to take orders. He had a sharp jaw that could've cut butter, olive-toned skin, dark hair smoothed back into a bun. These were such normal-looking people. While they had balked at the weirdo kid at the gas station, *these* people could have been any normal person on the street.

Jack sidled up next to Phil as he shifted through the crowd, scanning the outer walls.

"I don't see any exits..." Jack whispered. Noah leaned into him. He smelled like piss and vomit.

Phil jerked his chin to the left, where Jack noticed a door read EMPLOYEES ONLY.

"You think?"

Phil nodded. "For now, let's just lay low. We don't want to look suspicious or get picked out in case they find that woman's body. Just hang tight."

On the stage, a woman came from behind the left curtain, rolling out a table on which a man was strapped down. He had a bag over his head, but otherwise he was naked. Jack noted that an IV ran to his left arm, port laying on the bed beside him.

The woman pulled out a syringe and gave the man a hefty dose of something. His body tensed, muscles behaving erratically as they spasmed and twitched. Jack wished he could ask Phil what he thought the drug was, but he didn't want anyone to overhear them. He looked like he was being electrocuted, and the pale bag around his face grew gradually damp. Jack assumed he was frothing at the mouth. He was glad they couldn't see his face, his identity. Separating him from that individuality somehow made what was about to happen just a little easier to swallow.

The woman stripped down as she was joined by two other naked women, gathering around the man as he continued to convulse. Jack quickly realized they were pretending to be surgeons. The 'doctor' asked for tools, and the other girls passed them along.

The man was still alive but didn't fight back. Not even as the head woman flayed open his chest and abdomen, digging her hands into the warm blood of his abdominal cavity. She withdrew her drenched hands, and one of the nurses came to stand beside her, putting her hands onto her shoulder as they pressed their breasts together and the doctor fingered her with her bloody hand, leaving streaks of blood across her thighs.

The other nurse, left to her own devices, started cutting pieces off of the man, slivers of flesh and pieces that they could use for masturbation.

Noah had turned away, and Phil hadn't looked away for a moment. Jack was stuck somewhere in between their static opposites, eyes going to and from the horror on the stage: the somehow erotic display of violence and then back down to someone's threadbare tennis shoes; the girls getting off on each other's blood-lubed fingers and then the tag of some guy's shirt.

He had failed to notice until that very moment, however, that the crowd was really getting involved. Couples were making out all around them, and Jack was suddenly aware of the sounds of moans and screaming from the patrons of the theater.

"Phil," Jack whispered, "I think it's now or never. Security is distracted."

He motioned over to the two security guards that stood by the stage. Neither of them had their eyes on the crowd, and both held their cocks in their hands.

"Alright," Phil said, sweating beneath his mask. His eyes were bloodshot and vibrant. "Let's... where the fuck is Noah?"

Jack's heart sank, because of course if someone was going to fuck up their escape it would be fucking Noah. He spun around, eyes scanning the crowd of other masked people. Luckily most of them were attached to someone else, so he was looking for an outlier.

He finally saw Noah and his cat mask, backing away from the stage and crowd in pure horror. Jack took slow steps towards him, trying not to draw attention towards either one of them.

Two people were leaned against the bar having sex. The woman was slumped, back pressed against the wet wood surface as she arched away from the man who was sloppily humping *at* her (but probably not in her, Jack bet) as he struggled with the angle. Noah was backing up too quickly and not looking where he was going. He slammed his back against the man's.

The woman screamed, sitting bolt upright as she clawed at the man's back and grinded against him; Noah's collision had successfully sent him and his dick *right* where they needed to be.

The man, however, was not pleased and spun around, leaving his mistress panting on the bar-top as he spun Noah around by the shoulder and swung a fist into his face.

Jack had the opportunity to catch him as he fell away from the impact, but he'd sidestepped. Phil swept in, catching Noah in midair. Even more delirious than he had been from all of the drugs, Noah sputtered blood and broken teeth. The mask was fractured, shattered into pieces and embedded in his nose and cheek. A piece of slim plastic stuck out of the pink corner of his eye, and it bounced when he blinked away the blood.

"Now or never, now or never, let's *go*," Phil said, hauling Noah up like he was weightless, guiding him to the auditorium doors that led… somewhere.

Jack wasn't so sure that he wanted to go anywhere that was designated for the employees of this place, but they didn't have much of a choice. Phil walked with such a confidence that, initially, no one even tried to stop them.

13

PHIL'S HEART was in his throat. He had never really understood the phrase until that moment: he could feel the frantic pulsing as it beat in the back of his throat, threatening to gag him. He thought that if he opened his mouth, he might vomit the massive pulsing organ onto the floor. More than once, he wound his own hand around his neck, willing it to calm.

The wolfish mask helped to hide his worried complexion, green eyes betraying no sign of the crippling concern that he was feeling deep down.

"Come on, come on," he whispered to Noah. "Keep moving now."

The deafening music was quieter here, and the hallway was lit with regular light bulbs. It was somehow even more horrific in the faux-sterile white light. They were grimy and disgusting, like victims that had been trapped in rubble for hours. Phil recalled once when a couple of teenagers had fallen into a mine shaft and had to be rescued. It had taken hours, well into the night and into the next morning, for the rescue squad and paramedics to recover the living kids and the body of their less fortunate friend. When they had come into the light, they'd looked not too differently than the three men there in the hallway now.

Phil's head was throbbing too, worse now that they were in the harsh light. His skull felt like it was full of cotton, but something inside the fluffy mass of grogginess made a slow and consistent thud like a fist on a wooden door. He knew he had a concussion, and he could feel the weakness in his limbs. He was somehow sleepy, even in this impossible situation.

Jack must have noticed too, because he ducked his shoulder underneath Phil's free arm and hoisted him up. Jack smelled like shit and sweat and surprisingly a little bit of cologne. Phil remembered the kind, maybe. The blue glass bottle with the skinny neck: it smelled woody and citrusy. Damn good cologne to still be detectable and pleasant. They should put Jack in a commercial.

"I'm in bad shape," Phil admitted quietly. He didn't turn directly to look at Jack but saw his head nod and his Adam's apple bob as he swallowed. He knew Jack wasn't doing so hot either, and Noah…

He heard Jack speak, as though he'd read his mind: "Noah, you alright, man?"

Noah was dragging his feet as he walked, and they were a chain of arms and ragged bodies as they tried to support each other. The hall curved to the right ahead. Phil noted a set of older double doors, stained and scuffed. It looked like they did not match the rest of the building. There was a single door to their left, only a few feet away.

"Do you hear that?" Noah asked, voice high-pitched and panicked.

Phil strained through his own muffled hearing, and then he exchanged looks with Jack. He saw the same terror in his bloodshot eyes. There were people ahead of them, talking, and they were probably coming this way.

Phil dove for the door to the left, praying to God or whoever might be listening in a hell like this. The door was unlocked, he swung it open, motioning the other two men inside.

It was dark, and Phil fumbled for a light switch on the wall, fingers dragging across splintered studs, exposed wires, and uneven materials. He could tell the room was unfinished and under construction before he ever found the switch to turn on the lights. When it came on, it was a set of cheap yellow bulbs, and they made the room look so normal.

Other than the dead man in a metal lawn chair.

The man was stripped naked, and his skin had signs that he'd been beaten with something thin, maybe a whip or rope. Welts covered him, bruises pooled around the bottoms of his feet and his thighs. He'd been here a little while, Phil recognized. His penis had been amputated and his testicles were hanging out of his scrotum: dangling above the floor, shriveled and sticky-dry, by two ropes of tubular flesh.

"Shit," Phil whispered, peeling his eyes away from the corpse.

Jack pressed his hip into the door, ignoring the dead man, and slowly turned the lock as they heard the people in the hall pass by. Phil couldn't hear what they were saying, but Jack had his ear against the crack and seemed to be able to detect some of the conversation.

"They're looking for her," Jack said. "The woman in my room, I think. They said she didn't clock out."

Phil's mind was racing. He had killed someone; murdered someone. This woman who no doubt had a life outside of this place. He wondered if she had a spouse or kids, a day job, someone that had her coffee ready at the cafe every morning. He forced himself to stop thinking about it.

Noah made a quiet sound in his throat, "Oh, no, no, no…"

"Noah?" Phil asked, pushing his wolf mask onto the top of his head. Jack seemed to have just remembered he was also wearing his mask, and threw it to the floor.

Noah had started walking towards the corpse very slowly, bent at the knees like he was afraid it might jolt to life and scare him. He reached out to wipe away blood from the man's upper chest, his left shoulder where a faded tattoo lay. It was a spread-eagled female demon… anatomically correct.

"What is it, Noah?" Phil asked again, swallowing back nervousness.

"I know him," Noah admitted. "It's the guy."

Phil took a hesitant step towards Noah, squinting at the mangled face of the man in the chair. His face and body were so damaged that Phil couldn't be sure, but he didn't think he knew him.

"It's the guy I'm pretending to be: rainyday666. Roth."

"You don't know that," Phil whispered, spinning Noah around and wrapping his arms around him. It was the only thing he could think to do. Noah was cold and sweaty, entire body vibrating as though it were full of electricity. The moist coolness made Phil sick: it was like cold, dirty dishwater.

"You knew him? Like in real life?" Jack asked.

"No… I've never met him, but he posted about this stupid tattoo when he got it. How many douchebags would have a tattoo of a she-devil's hairy twat on their chest?"

Jack covered his face with his hands, breathing deeply into them. He was exhaling deeply through pursed lips, nearly whistling with every forced blow.

"You don't *know* though, Noah. You have no way to know for sure," Phil insisted.

"What does this mean?" Jack asked, the question overlapping.

Phil looked at Jack. He was a little surprised that he talked over him like that. Phil didn't have a superiority complex, not consciously anyway. Despite this, he had always taken up the role of the leader and had been given some degree of respect from Noah, and of course Jack always went with the flow. He was seeing now, however, a more feral side to their quiet friend. Jack would need his newfound sharp edge, Phil thought. Jack might not need Phil to drag him out of here after all.

Just as the consideration formed in his brain, however, Jack started crying. He leaned back against the door, sliding down slowly to the floor, grimacing in pain.

"How is this happening? How is this happening to *us*? We're good guys, aren't we? Just normal guys? I have a family," Jack insisted, eyes appearing suddenly pink-rimmed. It added an intense vibrancy to his baby blues. "I know it doesn't matter, in the grand scheme of things, if I fucking reproduced or not but... shit. I don't *deserve* this."

"Jack... Come on, man. Pull it together."

Jack looked up at him, eyes desperate. "If Noah's right, and that is the guy he's pretending to be... that means that they probably know we're lying. They're going to kill us. We're going to die here. We have been pawns in some kind of twisted game. They're playing with us."

Phil had a pang in his gut. It felt like he'd taken a literal punch that nearly toppled him over. He was walling off the fear of losing his family. He didn't dare think of it. He could look death right in the face, the prospect that he might die here. He wasn't afraid of that; maybe it wasn't real to him yet. He didn't know where the bravery came from. He didn't know why he had this solemn determination to get his friends out of there alive, and why he was willing to risk so much to keep them out of harm's way. It was just there.

He couldn't think of never seeing his family again though. Even knowing that after death he might have no awareness of that loss, he didn't think he could handle the possibility that he would know. The feeling that his family would have if he never came home. No one would ever find them here, or worse... They *would* find their bodies, and they'd know how they suffered.

"Just..." Phil started, closing his eyes to take a breath and try to collect himself. "You're not going to die here, Jack. I promise you."

"You can't promise me that."

"I just did," Phil confirmed, swallowing a lump in his throat. He forced a crooked, toothy smile. He rarely smiled with his teeth, the first premolar on the top left had a little chip in it that he'd always found a little unsightly.

Noah wrapped his arms around himself, squeezing tightly as he choked back his own tears.

"I'm already dead," he whispered.

Jack looked up at Noah, and Phil reluctantly followed suit.

"This is my life flashing before my eyes... I'm up to this point in the memory, I can feel it. We've already not made it. This is just the flashback. Just firing neurons."

Phil buried his face in his hands briefly, wiping away blood and sweat on his greasy palms. "We're going to make it. Get your mask, Jack. We might need it. Noah, we'll have to steal you one or something."

Noah wasn't listening. He continued to murmur, "We didn't make it, Phil."

14

As QUICKLY AS it had come on, Noah's wave of paranoia and panic subsided, pulling, dragging as it receded like a tide over sand. It was unsettling for him that those moments felt like they had the most clarity, like the rest of this, where he wasn't thinking the worst, was numbness and unreality. Somehow *not* being worried felt irresponsible, unrealistic, cold. Noah had, before tonight, been so very carefree and unbothered by anything. Now he couldn't stop stressing. He could feel it in every fiber of his being.

Noah stared straight ahead as Phil was taking the time to pull shards of the plastic mask out of his face. His left brow was split open and dangling onto his eyelid, but he was surprised at how little it hurt. Pieces of the mask had fractured when he'd been punched, and those chunks had embedded themselves into his nose and the plump flesh of his cheeks.

"This shit is sharp," Phil whispered. "Like fiberglass or something."

When Phil had done all he could, Noah took the biggest piece of the mask, which was still able to be worn, and stuck it into his pocket.

"I don't know if I can go back out there," Noah admitted.

It was Jack this time who turned to him. "We don't have a choice, Noah. It's just a matter of time before they find us here. We have to do everything we can to get out of here. We can't leave you behind. So… just come on, okay?"

Jack's voice was quiet, more characteristic of him. Since shit had hit the fan, Jack had become a little more hostile. Noah wasn't used to it. This was nice; having Jack back to himself was comforting. Noah felt a wave of calm flow over him.

"I'm up and down, guys. Up and down," Noah said. "I feel like I'm starting to come down, then I'll start tripping balls again."

"There's no telling how much shit you took," Phil said.

"How long have we been here?" Noah asked, almost afraid to do so.

Jack shrugged his shoulders and looked to Phil, who also shook his head. He responded quietly, "I'm not really sure. Maybe a couple of hours tops."

Noah closed his eyes tightly, nodding. So he still possibly had a few hours of the worst of it. Phil moved to the door, hand on the knob. He waited for a nod from both Noah and Jack, and then he turned off the lights and opened the door.

Noah trailed along the back, watching as Jack and Phil bumped shoulders to rush down the hall. They had so much confidence. Noah looked over his shoulder to make sure no one was following them, and then he hurried along behind.

Phil went straight for the double doors first, pushing one of them open. It needed more force than he'd expected, leaning his hip into it as the metal bottom scraped against the floor and echoed in the hall. A cool breeze hit Noah's ankles, a reminder that he was wearing his just-too-short acid-washed jeans. In any other situation the guys would be giving him hell about those pants and his exposed ankles over his stained white socks.

Noah leaned to the side to peer into the door with them. It appeared to be an old, unused addition to the theater. The adjoining wall was made of brick and had a fire escape that appeared to lead to an upper floor. The room was covered in decrepit furniture and building supplies.

"This wall here, the one made out of brick. I think this used to be outside. An exterior wall, I mean," Phil said quietly.

"Should we go look for an exit?" Jack responded.

"I don't think there is one. Unless we can get up the fire escape and go onto an upper level. We'd probably just be sitting ducks up there."

Noah shook his head. "I'm afraid of heights."

Phil nodded. "It's fine. Let's just go on down the hallway."

He let the door shut quietly, and Jack grabbed his elbow. Noah watched as Jack moved a finger up slowly to point in the corner of the ceilings where black half-spheres were mounted.

Cameras.

Noah felt like his paranoia was returning the moment he saw those things there, the red light barely visible behind the dark coverings. They would know they were in the hallway. They might be watching them now.

They took the section of hall that went to the right and found another small stretch ahead of them. Still no obvious exit. Noah was starting to worry that their only options were to go back into the main auditorium or to try to venture back to the front lobby.

Suddenly, they heard a door creak open. At first, Noah thought it might have been in his head: a sort of exaggerated sound that one would find in a horror movie. Jack and Phil heard it too, stopping in their tracks as a woman walked out of a room.

She wore a black dress that hung off of her shoulders and tall combat boots. She looked like she should've been wearing heels, Noah thought. She had on a fox mask that shined gold and red, bedazzled with more bling than the masks tucked away in their pockets.

"Gentlemen," she said, smiling at them. Her pouting red lips pulled up gently at the corners into a smile. "You seem to be a little lost…"

"We're just looking for the exit," Phil explained calmly. How did he do that? How did he reel in all of his fear and insecurity and concern to sound so casual? Yes, ma'am, I'd like a coffee with two creams and one *get us the fuck out of here.*

"Follow me," she said simply, walking back into the doorway from where she had been.

The men exchanged glances. Phil took a step forward and Jack spoke up, quietly, "I don't like this."

"Do we have a choice?" Phil asked back.

"Maybe we can just keep playing the part," Noah suggested. Jack reluctantly nodded, and they followed the woman into the room.

It was an office of sorts. A small room with a wood composite desk, a small row of bookshelves that housed more curios than books. There were two end tables on either side of the desk that were built better than the desk itself. Noah quickly realized that they were giant wooden dog crates, and each one in turn housed a massive dog. The canines watched as the men entered the room, yellow and amber eyes glowing from the shadows. They had meaty bones between their front paws. The doors, thankfully, were latched shut.

Jack flinched when he noticed them, causing Noah to run into him. Jack hated dogs, they all knew that. Phil had a goofy, old golden retriever named Navy. She was gray muzzled with worn down, brown teeth. The front ones showed between her sagging lips in a permanent smile. She popped and cracked when she walked and couldn't hear anything except the can opener anymore. Despite the fact that she was the most non-threatening dog on the planet, Jack would always argue that anything with teeth, no matter how decayed and worn, could bite.

Jack recovered surprisingly well, entering the room and choosing the seat in the center, so that he was not close to either dog.

There were those three chairs, almost as though she'd been expecting three guests. *That's just paranoia. Calm down. Do not start freaking out right now and blow your cover. Chill out,* Noah thought.

Noah took the seat to Jack's left, and Phil placed himself in the remaining chair.

The woman came to sit on the desk, uncomfortably close to them. She crossed one leg over the other, boot dangerously close to Jack's chin. He didn't even flinch but instead stared directly at her. Noah thought he could see something venomous in Jack's eyes. Something unlike him that he had been noticing since they'd realized this place was a madhouse. It was like he was possessed, and every so often a shadow of that thing passed behind his eyes and threatened to surface.

"So, who are the three of you?" she asked, still donning her fox mask as she looked at each of them one at a time.

Phil stammered, "Well, we're... You see, we're just..."

Jack's eyes darted to Noah, who scooted to the edge of the seat and said, "I'm Roth."

The fox lady's face turned from Phil to Noah in such a slow and direct movement that it looked mechanical. Her eyes twinkled, glittering with mischief.

"Oh, are you Mr. Roth?" her voice chimed, excited and vibrant. White teeth shone like fangs behind her red lips, wet and slick.

"I am," Noah said, straining to keep his voice steady.

"That's interesting. I seem to remember a Mr. Roth, but... I can't quite put my finger on it..."

She moved to the edge of the desk, leaning down to hover her face only inches from Noah's. He tried to maintain eye contact with her, but through his peripheral he could see Jack and Phil shift nervously.

Her face was becoming slowly dynamic, rippling underneath, like someone moving a movie screen from behind. *Not now, not now.* He could smell bourbon on her breath and the slightest hint of her feminine deodorant. He felt like the skin on his skull was sagging, and he wished he would melt straight through the bottom of the chair and away from this situation.

"Don't you recognize me?" she asked, lip puckering.

Noah mouthed the word 'what,' but no sound left his throat. He shook his head instead from side to side, focusing on her so intensely to try and decide where he may have seen her before... he went cross-eyed in the desperate attempt.

"What? Doesn't the mask give it away?" she pressed towards him even more, uncrossing her legs and pressing a knee between his legs to rest on the chair. He tried too late to clamp his knees together, trapping her knee between his thighs as he tried to keep her from advancing towards him. He felt her press against his crotch, and it made his gut wrench.

"Who?" he whispered, feeling tears stinging his eyes.

"Is it the wig? Should I have worn black?" She reached up and pushed her mask off of her face, tossing it onto the desk. It clattered and Noah jumped, spine jammed against the back of the chair so hard that he could feel it grind. She went on, "Does Vixxn ring a bell?"

"No. No, no, no, no," Noah squealed, putting a hand over his mouth.

Noah stole a glance to his friends for comfort. Jack's face was devoid of any color, bleached bone-white. Phil was tense, hands gripping the side of his chair so tightly that his biceps bulged against the sleeves of his shirt. He looked ready to move.

She laughed, the sound rolling into a purr. "I knew you'd show up. Noah, is it? Such an annoying troll. Keyboard warrior. They always act so big and bad, but you get them in a situation with real horror, real pain, real confrontation... and they just fall apart. Fall to pieces."

"You can't tell us you just lure in internet trolls to torture them," Phil snapped. "There's no way."

"Not our primary audience, no. Sometimes we just need a little fodder for the fire, a little something fun, and I decided if I was going to get Mr. Roth in here I might as well see if I could snag Noah too. Poetic in a way, the two of you here together after your little text altercation." She turned her attention back to Noah, moving in even closer. Her breath felt like scalding steam on his skin. "I just didn't think you'd bring friends... but the more, the merrier."

Phil spoke again, seeming to be the only one brave enough to address her. "Why would you, as a woman, put other women through this kind of torture? What is wrong with you?"

She laughed. "You don't get to try to act like an advocate for women here, honey. Don't act like you didn't come here with intentions of getting your dick wet. You did, didn't you? I'm simply supplying a demand, and everyone, including you, darling, have *demanded* this. This is what the people want. There are plenty of men ordered daily for rooms, I am an equal opportunity supplier. I brought you here, didn't I? Do you want to know how many men and women we dispose of every month? I keep immaculate records. There are trends you know."

"You're sick. This place and all of these people are sick."

Vixxn laughed and then turned back to Noah, leaning down. "I'm sorry that the experience wasn't up to your standards, Noah. I'm afraid there are no refunds. But you asked if you could leave... absolutely. *Absolutely.* In a box. Or a bag. I can be flexible."

Noah hadn't breathed the entire time she had spoken. He could feel his face gathering heat, eyes burning, but his limbs felt so cold. She snapped towards Noah like she would have bitten him in the face and he jerked away, but Phil was on his feet and rushing towards her.

He punched her in the side of the head so hard that she toppled over one of the dog crates and landed on the floor behind the desk. The dogs started barking, clawing against the doors of their cage as spittle flew between the bars.

"Run!" Phil yelled, and the three of them stumbled over their chairs and out the door.

Noah struggled to keep up, legs becoming heavy as he heard the woman scream like she was boiling over with anger. He could feel the sound wrack his bones, sending stabbing pain through his entire body. The dogs continued to bark, and then he could hear the sound of their nails on the floor as they were released.

15

JACK RAN AHEAD of Phil and Noah, sneakers squeaking on the floor as he skidded around the corner back the way they'd come. Noah had fallen behind, struggling to breathe as Phil hauled him up and not only supported him but pushed him ahead.

As he rounded the corner, he saw two security guards standing between him and the door back to the theater auditorium. One had on a white rabbit mask with mismatched ears, and the other had on a bear. Jack stumbled backwards, fumbling as he collided with his friends. Phil jerked open the stubborn door to the old room behind them, ushering them inside.

It smelled like dust, mothballs, mildew. There was a collapsing theater, furniture covered in draped white cloths, and a decrepit piano. Jack stood in place for several moments, confused and lost. Where should they go now? No glowing exit signs, no doors that seemed to lead anywhere. They could climb onto the stage and try to go through the dressing rooms in hopes that there was a window... *anything*.

He heard Noah scooting a bench against the door and turned to see him shoving a broom shaft between the handles of the doors.

Phil grabbed a handful of Jack's shirt and nearly pulled him off of his feet. He spun around, propelled forward as he was pushed towards the fire escape. Phil squatted down, cupping his hand to give Jack a boost up. The ladder was several feet off the ground, hanging in the air.

"You go first, Phil," Jack insisted.

"Shut up, Jack. You can't boost Noah up. Go on in case he can't pull himself up." Phil was sweating again, face flushed pink, vein bulging in his neck as he hoisted Jack up.

Even lifted, Jack struggled to grab onto the elevated ladder, finding where it was hanging off of a rusted track on one side. It seemed held in place by rust alone. He blinked away debris as particles of rust fell into his eyes. He found the strength to haul himself up the ladder, going up until he was on the platform. It creaked with his weight, and Jack found himself unable to get up onto his feet for fear it would fall.

He watched as Phil struggled with Noah, who was not only much heavier than the two of them but also exhausted and panicking. He somehow managed to lift him, nearly tossing him into the air. And, thank God, Noah managed to grab onto the ladder and somehow start climbing.

"Come on, Phil!" Jack insisted, shrilly, watching as the door rattled and budged as someone slammed against it from the outside.

Phil sprinted across the room and pulled a large plastic garbage can over, turning it upside down as he spilled the contents and scrambled on top of it. He barely had enough height to jump and grab the ladder, but he was coming. He nearly caught up with Noah, chest hovering above the same rung as his friend's feet. Jack hurried them on, slamming his palms against the platform as the door flew open and the two dogs burst in.

As Noah pushed off the top step of the escape ladder, Jack hoisted him up and heard a clang followed by a raucous scraping.

Then the screams.

Phil was not coming up the ladder after them, and he was screaming in a way that didn't suit him. It wasn't a sound you would have expected from the man, or from any man. It muted into gurgling sobs muddled with cuss words and spittle.

Jack and Noah rushed over to the edge to find that the ladder had fallen down part of the way, and Phil's feet were dangling six or so feet from the ground.

"Climb up!" Noah squealed, reaching down desperately with his good hand. His fingertips grappled in the air, much too far away for Phil to grab.

That was when Jack noticed that Phil's hand was wedged between the ladder and the damaged track behind it. Phil must have grabbed between the gap for leverage at just the wrong time. The only reason the ladder had stopped where it had was because it had jammed with the now mutilated flesh and bone of Phil's left hand wedged between. Blood poured in pregnant, laboring drops onto the ground below. One finger looked like it had been torn off entirely, bone splintered through the skin like pieces of teased feather. The others were a single, bloody, purple mass between the two pieces of metal.

The dogs were barking, and Jack's heart raced.

"I know it hurts, Phil, but you have got to at least try," Jack begged, hands clenching into fists as he banged them against the metal platform again.

Phil's face was red, beading with sweat. He puffed air in his cheeks, exhaling them between pursed lips. Noah scrambled to the side of the building, pulling off broken pieces of brick as he went to the edge to prepare to hurl them at the approaching dogs.

Vixxn strolled behind the vicious canines, a casual walk with a playful swing of her hips. Like a true horror villain, Jack thought. She didn't have to run to keep up. They were doomed; even as she walked, taking her time, and they ran for their lives... she would catch up. She would win. They weren't going to get a sequel.

Phil seemed reinvigorated by the appearance of the dogs and reached up with his other hand to try and pull himself onto the ladder. He managed to lift his body up enough to get the crook of his elbow in one step, taking a breath before he tried to reach up for the next step. As he reached, his elbow lost its traction, and he dropped. The pain had him screaming again, and he grappled to hang on to the lower step to relieve the tension on his mangled fingers.

Then the ladder gave way again. Two fingers severed themselves from his hand, falling to the ground, and the stairs dropped another two feet. One dog took the fingers into his slim maw, crunching them excitedly as he looked up, saliva pouring down the sides of his neck. The second dog flew into the air like he was weightless, teeth barely grazing the bottom of Phil's left foot. He tucked his legs up as high as he could, looking up and yelling for help.

"Jesus fucking Christ, somebody help me!" Phil screamed as one of the dog's clamped onto his ankle, hanging there. Its body lurched and jerked as it slung its head around to try and tear flesh. He was actually screaming, screaming like Jack had never heard anyone scream before. It was a terrible, grating and unreal sound. His voice was breaking, gargling. He was crying. Phil never begged, never asked for anything. He never cried, never raised his voice unless at the television during an intense game. There was no emotion left there, nothing human. It was primordial, desperate: a vinyl record left on loop long after the tracks were done. Just white noise, an ancient emptiness, the paradoxical silence.

Noah was sitting with his knees pulled up to his chest, hands clamped over his ears as he tried to muffle the sound of his friend being torn apart.

Phil's noise reduced more and more, until you heard more of the dogs than anything. Jack stole a glance over the side, seeing that Phil had been successfully torn apart, arm swelling where his elbow had released and dislocated, foot and calf on his right leg totally disassembled. The dogs were stretching and tattering him like a rag doll. The mangled hand finally gave way at the wrist, remaining lodged but allowing Phil's still gasping body to fall away. The dogs were on his face in an instant, tearing his throat out. Air wheezed out of his windpipe, spraying blood into the air before he effectively drowned in his own blood. One dog grabbed onto Phil's head, chewing around with a crunch, tongue lolling around the corners of its cheeks as it tasted the fluid that poured from the skull like a cracked fruit hull. The other dog had taken off with one of his bloody shoes, delivering it to Vixxn with a wildly wagging tail.

Jack reached down, jerking Noah onto his feet.

"We have to go now. We have to go right now."

Noah's eyes looked swollen, and he squinted at Jack as he blew spit bubbles and tried to say something. Jack just shook his head, feeling his own throat constrict as he let himself cry too. He took Noah's hand and dragged him along, running on the unsteady platform as they reached the door at the end. Jack took a shaking breath, entire body quivering. He turned the knob slowly, nervously, and it opened.

16

NOAH HAD LOST his voice screaming. Rather, he considered that his voice could be lost somewhere... He thought about where a voice might go when it is 'lost.' He wondered who could hear his sobbing wails, and if they cared.

Nothing but a rasp was coming out of his throat as he trailed along behind Jack, but the sound he was trying to make was heavy in his chest. He had never seen anyone die before today. He thought nothing could have felt worse than seeing the red-headed woman as Phil had beaten her to death with the vibrator, but she had died so quietly. Other than those final gasps for life, she had not made a sound.

He could not stop hearing Phil's screams. He knew by now that Phil was long gone, but it was like the sound echoed in his head. The way he had begged them to help him. He had always put their safety first, their wellbeing before his. In those moments they had left him there scared and in pain. He could feel the dogs tearing away the flesh on him, shattering and crunching bone, scoring fabric with their teeth. Every sound left Noah with intense physical pain, nausea, and the cold and bitter flavors of metal and coffee.

They were in some kind of old attic. They had thought it was clear that the old auditorium was out of use, but this room had even less life to it. There were boxes of old film reels, although this appeared to be more of a performance theater overall. There were racks of dusty, sequined costumes and dresses, piles of cobweb-covered wigs. The floor was all but lined with newspapers.

"What's the plan?" he managed to croak.

Jack stopped, turning to look back at him. His own eyes were bloodshot, face streaked with tears. The muscles in his jaw were taut and bulging through his slim cheeks. Noah thought he could hear his teeth squeak together.

"I don't know… Fuck if I know," Jack said, falling against a wall before he slid to the floor, his knees folded up towards his chest like a neatly-manufactured chair.

"Do you think we can just… hide here until they close?"

Did a place like this close? Where did they keep all of the people? The victims? He wondered if there was a lower level, like a makeshift dungeon where people were lined up in cells and fed gruel through a slot in the door. Or maybe they shuffled them in with vans through the back door, pulling up to the delivery dock before they unloaded them like cattle bound for slaughter… but that would be too risky. Traveling on any major highway with prisoners in the backseat, you could get pulled over for a minor traffic violation and end up with a serious issue on your hands. Unless maybe they didn't use major roads at all, which led him to the thought that…

"There will be someone here all hours, I'm sure." Jack's raspy voice interrupted his thoughts. He didn't sound like himself, voice as grating as a chain-smoker's. "Even if we get out of here, where are we going to go? Maybe we could cut through the woods… less likely for someone from here to see us that way…"

"Can't we take…" Noah swallowed. He was afraid to say his name, like it was suddenly a harbinger of bad juju. He took a shaking breath through his nostrils, sucking snot down the back of his throat. "Phil's van? Can't we take the van? I remember where he parked it."

Jack shook his head, not making eye contact. "The keys; they're in his pocket."

The realization hit Noah like a physical wall. He jerked his head back, blinking wildly. He had somehow not even thought of the keys, of the fact that they'd need them to unlock and drive the van. So it had not even occurred to him where the keys were. Somewhere in that mess of tattered flesh and fabric that was once a man, probably being turned into a pile of dog shit, lay their only realistic escape route. That stupid key, wrapped in pink from one of those machines at the store, with a scuffed up keyfob and a leopard print 'T' keychain complete with a teal pompom.

"What about his family?" Noah asked quietly. "What do we tell them?

Jack looked up at Noah then, eyes boring into his. Noah took a step backwards, heart wrenching at the way his friend was regarding him. He tried to tell himself it was just the drug-induced paranoia, and not reality. There is no way that Jack, the guy who never got flustered or upset about anything, could be looking at him with such pure hatred. Jack would blush when you suggested he was angry, or when he was embarrassed or flustered. Jack just didn't hate. Jack didn't give people looks like this.

"The odds of us getting out of here are next to zero," Jack finally said, leaning over to tie his shoe. He winced as he did so, as though something hurt. Noah knew the adrenaline was probably wearing down, and eventually the pain it had been hiding would surface for both of them. Even as Noah blinked, the flap of his eyebrow flopped around in his line of sight.

"We have to get out of here... I can't die here. I don't want to die here," Noah said. The words sounded pathetic when they came out of his mouth, and he recognized that. He knew that Jack had no control over where Noah died.

"Do you think Phil wanted to die here?"

Noah opened his mouth to respond, but no words came out. *This is all my fault.*

"This is your fault," Jack said, parroting Noah's thought.

It hurt to hear him say it for some reason. His gut twisted into knots, his chest felt tight. Even when he wholly believed it himself, hearing it from the lips of his friend made it hit differently.

"Do you think he wanted to die like that?"

"No. He didn't deserve it. I never…"

Noah couldn't hold back crying anymore. Tears were gone, his eyes were dry, and his chest ached with the effort. His body wanted to sob but he couldn't.

Jack's face twisted, mouth corkscrewing towards his nose. Noah had to look away as his face started to look like liquid spiraling down a drain. He could almost hear the gurgling sound. He took deep breaths, pinching himself in the soft part of his arm, using the pain to ground him.

"I'm sorry, Noah," he gasped, putting his hands over his mouth. "I know you would never get us into this on purpose. I know that."

Noah didn't feel better about it. Even if the intentions had not been malicious, and even if he had been ignorant to the whole thing, it was still his fault they were there. If he hadn't been so determined to one up them, to *impress them,* they wouldn't be here.

If he could get out of here he would never troll anyone online again. Hell, he'd never get on the internet again. Ever. He would happily tell everyone he was a pussy and he didn't want to experience anything like the real thing. He wasn't even sure he would watch or read horror again.

Noah couldn't stop thinking about Phil's family either. How would they react to the news of Phil's death? Would the media paint him as a villain? He wished he could survive to tell them how Phil tried to save them, and how he had put their safety first. He wouldn't tell them how he had begged for them to help him in the end, and how they had been unable to save him. He hoped they never learned about this place at all. Not knowing was better than knowing this ugly reality.

Then something terrible dawned on him, something he didn't want to think about.

"What about our wallets? They kept our IDs and everything, our phones. What if they go after Phil's family or..."

Noah didn't have to finish what he was going to say, he could tell from the look on Jack's face that he realized what Noah was suggesting. If they wanted to, these people could go straight to their houses.

"We have to get to the lobby then," Jack said, standing up with a newfound determination. "We have to get our stuff, Phil's stuff."

"There's no way we can get down there without them seeing us. They're looking *for* us now."

Noah suddenly wished he hadn't said anything to Jack.

Jack started walking again, and Noah tried to catch up. The floor creaked beneath his feet, threatening to give. There was a door there, bolted from the inside, that Jack unlocked and swung open. Then without hesitation he started descending down a musty-smelling staircase.

Noah paused at the top, watching his friend descend into darkness.

17

Jack was going with or without Noah. He headed down the stairs with such speed that he nearly tripped if not for the railing on the right wall. His entire body was ice cold, frosty and crispy-feeling as his hair stood on end against the rising bumps on his flesh. He had not considered that they might go after his family. As though this situation could not have gotten more serious, now Jack felt like there was nothing he would not do. He did not have any restraints now.

His children, as cliché as it may sound, meant more to him than anything in the world. If he had to choose between his children and his wife, he would use her as a fucking human shield to protect them. And he *loved* his wife. They had a good marriage, a solid friendship. They were balanced. He wasn't sure how long that would last—monogamy in humans did seem so unnatural—but Jack could honestly never think of a time that he'd actually considered cheating on her or leaving her. He'd like to think she felt the same way. He could imagine these terrible people sneaking into his home and doing terrible things to her and to his kids, things worse than murder. He could not let that happen; he *would not* let that happen.

He heard Noah coming after him, whimpering. He felt guilty

about being a dick to him, because he knew he was struggling. Noah normally was not this whiny and needy, and Jack reminded himself that he was overloaded with drugs and stress. Jack had never done drugs, although he had pretended to partake a few different times with Phil and Noah in college, no one ever knew the difference. Or if they did they didn't say anything. He didn't know what being under the effects of hallucinogenics was like, but he knew that as much as Noah had taken could not be safe... and the effects would not be as desired. He imagined if he was in a torture porn version of *Fear and Loathing* he might be sobbing uncontrollably too. Was it like the movies with cartoon characters coming out of the walls and shit?

At the bottom of the stairs, Jack noticed a piece of faded paper behind a dusty piece of plexiglass on the wall. He used his bare arm to wipe away the cobwebs and sawdust, and beneath the covering he saw a water-damaged, moldy fire evacuation map. Jack leaned into the wall, squinting in the dark at the mottled black and green paper. This must have been the old layout of the theater, because he could tell certain portions that they had ventured through were missing from the plan. The auditoriums, the hallway, and the lobby, however, appeared to be original.

If he was following this correctly, they were standing right at the auditorium where the girls had been on stage. Noah was suddenly behind him, wheezing into his ear. Jack was overcome with the sour reek of body odor, vomit, and old piss.

"Back up," Jack snapped at him over his shoulder, squeezing his hands into fists. "I'm just... I'm on edge right now."

"I get it," Noah insisted. "I do. I'm sorry."

But he didn't back up.

"This is an old building fire evacuation map... thing. This door should lead us to the auditorium where the bar is. So... mask on."

"Mine's broken."

"It's better than nothing, put it on."

Jack struggled to get the beak out of his pocket, putting the bluejay mask back onto his face and watching as Noah's broken cat mask rested cockeyed on his nose. Jack reached up to adjust it for him, and Noah smiled. Something kind and generous that Jack had been shoving down into the depths of his soul fluttered. It didn't last long though.

He unlocked the deadbolt on the door and pushed it open. He could feel Noah leaning into his back and he nearly shoved him, but instead resorted to jerking his shoulder away.

They weren't *in* the auditorium as expected, but rather what appeared to be backstage. The area was set up like some sort of dressing room, and the smell of cigarettes and weed flooded Jack's nostrils.

He could hear voices, women talking amongst themselves. It was a light sort of conversation, so he assumed it wasn't Vixxn. He peered around the door slowly, eyes adjusting to the light, and then he caught sight of three girls sitting lazily in chairs as they smoked. They were all completely naked, perfectly relaxed and unaffected by each other's nudity.

And they saw him, too.

Jack started to slip back into the stairwell, but as his mind raced through the possible escape routes he realized that there was nowhere to go. Upstairs they would eventually be sitting ducks. No way in or out unless they went this way, or back to the platform where Phil had died. The women chose for him, because they were on their feet in an instant. He could hear them yelling 'hey!' and then approaching. He shut the door and looked back at Noah, breathless.

"We have to do this. You have to do this. I have to do this."

That was all that Jack could say before he shoved all of his body weight into the door, slinging it open and hitting one of the girls so hard that it sounded like a bat hitting a baseball: *plink!*

She stumbled, falling backwards over a chair. Another one of the girls, pale-skinned and covered in tattoos, came at him with something shining and silver. Before Jack could recognize that it was a scalpel, the same one she had likely used on stage, she had stabbed him in the shoulder with all of her strength. It was in the meaty part, right below his collar bone. He heard it pop through the flesh and muscle, and blood spurted wildly. He slung her arm away from him, and the handle of the scalpel clattered against the opposite wall, but the blade was buried inside his flesh.

A blonde girl had rushed to a red phone that was hanging on the wall, dialing a couple of numbers. It was one of those old-school phones with a wire and cord. Jack recalled when he and Phil had gotten a job at a warehouse in Whitebranch when they were young, they had a similar phone setup. It only operated inside the building and could connect you to other phones throughout: you just dialed an extension. It required no phone service, and was internal only with no external access.

He remembered Phil had used the phone once to have phone sex with this girl named Amber who worked down in the office. Amber was petite and curvy, probably five foot max. She dressed like she was going to a conservative church every day: layers of clothes and vests on sweaters or shawls over a blouse with pencil skirts and hosiery or just pants. This was deceptive though, because she had a thing for Phil and apparently she was *wild*. Jack had always been into her, but he was this tall and lanky weirdo with a mop of shaggy hair, a smattering of acne, and obsession with band t-shirts.

Phil had bragged about how the act was fun because just anyone could pick up the phone and hear them, Amber thought it was hot and dangerous. Little did Phil know, Jack had snuck off to one of the rooms where they kept stacks of pallets, picking up the line and tucking it against his shoulder as he'd feverishly jacked off, struggling to be quiet as Amber moaned and breathed into the receiver.

The tattooed girl was already back on him, shoving her thumb into his new wound. Pain emanated from the slit in his flesh, and the deeper she bore into him the further its tendrils of noxious sensation spread. He found himself screaming, but the sound rolled off into a snarl of determination as he struggled against her, grabbing ahold of her wrist and twisting it. She was growling back at him, still flinging herself at him, grabbing handfuls of flesh and hair whenever she could to try and throw him off.

"Noah!" Jack demanded. "The phone! Stop her!"

Noah was sliding with his back against the wall like the floor was lava, inching around Jack as he fought with the woman. He finally made his way over to the blonde, pulling on her elbow as he begged her to stop. He tried to tug the phone out of her hand. He was asking her, *fucking asking her to stop*. What the hell was wrong with him?

"Please, don't do this. We don't want to hurt anybody. We're just trying to get out of here," Noah pleaded, spittle pouring down his chin, his shoulders were hunched submissively, knees bent. The woman jerked away from him, she had a white knuckled grip on the phone. Her eyes darted from Noah to Jack.

The girl who had been knocked down by the door was back on her feet now, and came at Noah with a folded chair. She hit him in the back of the legs, aiming for his knees. It knocked him down and almost into the blonde. He rolled onto his backside, holding his hands up as he tried to fend her off. She hit him again over the back and his arms. Beating the shit out of him like a wrestler with a steel chair.

Jack knew he had to take action when the blonde started talking on the phone. He couldn't hear what she was saying. She was babbling and there was so much commotion in the room that it seemed whoever she had called was also having trouble understanding her. Jack was sure she was telling someone they were there, and it wouldn't take them long to get to them.

He looked down at the girl pressed against him, her dark eyes boring into his. Veins in her throat, coated with the rich black ink in the shape of skulls and flowers, popped as she used all of her strength to keep him pinned where he was against the door. Jack growled, shoving her and following her to the ground at first. She was stunned, blinking up at him in surprise, his blood was splattered all over her face and bare breasts. Bright, fat drops of scarlet.

Jack raised his knee to his chest, and stomped down on her face.

He was surprised at how much resistance there was to the structure of a face and skull. The way that on his first stomp, although he had put all of his effort into it, it still retained some sort of normal shape. He felt a stone bruise swelling up in the arch of his foot from the impact. The girl started to choke on her own teeth, nose crunched into a pulpy mass. She gurgled, too stunned to move as he continued to stomp her face into the floor. She finally rolled over, gasping as she tried to crawl away.

One well-placed kick to the back of her head, and she fell face down. She was unmoving and quiet, a large puddle of blood formed on the floor underneath her, spreading along the wooden planks like a pool of dark oil.

Jack was surprised at how he didn't feel anything. His heart was pounding so hard that he felt lightheaded, barely able to breathe deeply enough to sustain himself, but he didn't *feel* anything. There was no remorse, no guilt, no question. He had no doubt or moral dilemma. He was at peace with what he'd just done, and he needed to ride it out before he grew conscious again.

Noah had spun around and jerked the chair away from the girl that was hitting him, then he used it to shove her. She stumbled backwards, falling into a support beam and hitting the back of her head. Jack thought she'd be down for the count now, so he went straight for the blonde girl on the phone, shoving Noah out of the way to get to her.

He jerked the entire phone off of the wall, it bounced on the floor and left a small scuff of red paint. Noah covered his ears at the toll of the bell inside it.

Jack grabbed the cord and wrapped it around the girl's neck four times, pulling it so tight that she fell backwards towards him, bare buttocks pressing against him. He found himself pulling her closer, eyes drawn to her lips as they paled, then turned the lightest shade of blue.

"Jack, stop," Noah whispered quietly.

Jack didn't look at him, instead he looked at the girl who had hit her head. She was struggling to her feet, disoriented and stumbling. She used her hands to try and steady herself, scampering out of the room like a baby deer as she screamed for help.

"Go get her," Jack yelled to Noah, fingers going numb from the effort he was putting on the springy cord against the woman's throat. Noah wasn't going after her.

Jack spun around, pulling the cord back and putting it into Noah's hands.

"Do *not* let go. Do you understand me?"

Noah twisted the cord, his swollen lower lip puckered the smallest amount, "Jack, I can't. I can't."

"You can and you will," Jack demanded.

Jack sprinted after the final girl, catching up to her easily. She was stumbling, words slurred. Urine trickled down her thighs. For a woman who had stood on stage and participated in murder in front of dozens of masked psychopaths, Jack thought she would have had a strong enough constitution to avoid pissing herself.

He tackled her in the empty room, his shoes squeaking on the sticky floor as they struggled against each other. Her screams echoed around them. The auditorium had excellent acoustics for this type of thing.

Jack beat her until his knuckles were swelling. He'd never so much as punched anyone in his life. He had never hit anyone in any capacity, because he was mostly a pacifist, a mediator. If he could avoid a confrontation, he would. Even if it meant taking the blame or admitting defeat. Jack had been punched once. Only once. He was at a bar with Noah and Phil in Whitebranch, a little place called The Spigot. At the time Phil had a girlfriend over there that he was visiting, and he took them along for fun. Some local guys had gotten into a heated verbal argument with Noah over a game of darts, and it turned physical. Phil had intervened and a fight had ensued. Jack had tried to break it up, but when one of the locals decked him straight in the nose he'd ducked into the bathroom until it was over. His nose was a little crooked from the blow. Even then, he hadn't hit the guy back.

But he beat that woman to death.

He didn't remember doing it, he could not piece together the brief moments, seconds, that it had taken for him to kill her. He had burning scratches on his throat and his chin, blood dripped off of the blue arches of the mask, leaving a tinge of flavor on his lips. He got to his feet and stumbled away from her, delirious, drunk with adrenaline.

His hands hurt, the claw marks on his flesh hurt. His boxers were wet and tacky. He tried not to think about it, and didn't look at her.

It felt like it took him forever to get back onto the stage and into the dressing room behind the curtain. He was coming down from the excitement, and his body was begging him to slow down and rest. He wanted to sleep, his eyelids feeling heavy... like he could sleep in a place like this.

Noah was sitting on the floor, cradling the now-dead girl who had tried to use the phone. The cord was still tangled in her blonde hair and wound around her throat. He clutched her against his chest, rocking her like she was a child. He had his face buried in her hair, stroking the strands gently between his fingers as he sobbed that he was sorry over and over. As he kissed her forehead, Jack noticed her blue eyes were staring directly at him, unblinking. The pupils had released unevenly, mismatched, like the damaged apertures of a camera lens. Her sclera were splotched with blossoms of pink and red from ruptured vessels, intensifying the vibrant green of her irises.

Jack broke eye contact with her, and he stepped across the bodies of the two women and picked up their lighter off of the table. Noah clutched the naked woman tighter, as though he would somehow protect her from Jack now. A knot formed in Jack's throat as he looked down at his friend, considering what this meant for Noah and what it meant for him. It wasn't something he wanted to think about, but in this type of situation, sometimes you have to do the difficult thing.

Jack accepted it: Noah didn't have what it was going to take to get out of here.

18

THE HALLWAY WAS SURPRISINGLY QUIET, like everyone had left the premises. There were no friendly hostesses, no other patrons, and all of the masked party-goers seemed to have disappeared entirely. Noah found this somehow even more frightening. Wouldn't it be ridiculous if all of this was just a bad, bad trip from all of the drugs? Wouldn't that be *so amazing* if he just woke up in the hospital and it was all a bad fantasy? Jack would have snuck him in fast food and snack cakes. Phil would be there too, alive and in one piece. He would have bought him flowers as a gag, and he would laugh when he told him about everything that happened. They would all laugh about this fucked up horror orgy and murder brothel that Noah had dreamed up.

The happy dream sequence was shattered too quickly. Phil was dragging half of his body inside, struggling to close the door behind him with his one arm. His intestines left a bloody streak on the floor, squeaking as he dragged himself to the foot of the bed. He smiled, reaching forward to offer Noah a bouquet of gore and eyeballs. They rolled and glared at him. Jack was strapped to the wall, naked, bleeding. He didn't respond to them. Phil opened his mouth to speak, but all that came out was the cacophony of snarling dogs and Phil's own dying screams. Phil's jaw dropped unrealistically, unhinging and bobbing like the mouth of a ventriloquist's dummy as the noise droned on and on.

"Noah!" Jack barked.

Noah blinked, and suddenly he could see the red hall again. The loud music was throbbing in his chest.

"You alright? Hang in there," Jack yelled over the noise.

"I'm… I'm fine," Noah said quietly. He knew his voice was lost to Jack, but they continued on anyway.

Jack was having to drag him down the hall. He wished he could just get his body to cooperate with him, but he was done. He was exhausted. He had nothing left. He wasn't even sure he had the motivation to live anymore. What was after this? Could there possibly be a happily ever after? Could you go back to 'normal' after experiencing something like this?

Noah had killed that woman. Jack had made him do it, and he knew that they hadn't had much of a choice, but it still didn't feel right. It didn't feel necessary. Everything happened so fast. He would think about her for the rest of his life. He could feel her life leave her body, the way the room seemed more empty… how he felt more empty.

Jack went from being the quiet, pushover, house-husband flunky to murdering three women in what had to be record time. He hadn't even blinked; he'd just killed them with his hands. Noah didn't want to take credit for choking one of them to death while Jack… did whatever he'd done to the running woman.

At this point Noah thought the two of them deserved whatever was coming to them.

Jack stopped at the room where he had been tortured, opening the door and slipping inside. Noah followed suit, blinking as he looked around in the dim room. The straps that had held Jack still hung in the middle of the room. He saw that the redhead was still laying in the far corner, wadded up beside her bag of sex toys. Jack was on his knees, scooting his hands along the floor on the opposite side of the room.

Noah heard people outside the door, and his heart sank. He backed up into the darkness, clinging again to the wall. Anything to keep him on his feet, grounded.

"Jack," Noah whispered.

Jack looked up, putting a finger to his lips as he too heard the people in the hallway. Noah noticed then that Jack had a gun in his hand. It took him several moments to remember where the gun had come from. It was the same one that the redhead had pointed at him and Phil when they'd come to rescue Jack. She hadn't fired it. Was it real? Was it loaded? How many bullets did it have in it? Cartridges. Ammo. Noah didn't know anything about guns, they made him nervous. Did Jack know how to use a gun? How had they forgotten it? Phil always thought of everything. How had he forgotten the gun when it could have been their surefire way out of the building?

Suddenly the voices were passing by the door. They heard a brief exchange between two men.

"Let's get the rooms cleaned up," one man said. "I'm starving."

"Supposed to be on the lookout for those guys, you know. That's why they sent everybody off."

"Yeah, well, I figure they're already out. If not, they'll show up. Just some average Joes. Should go down pretty quiet."

"The director said to try to use the dogs if possible. Makes it easier to dump them off somewhere and make it look like an animal attack."

"Yeah, well, I'm not hauling one of those mutts around with me while I clean."

"Yeah, let's just get this done, alright?"

"Okay, I'll take this one. I'll meet you in the breakroom when I'm done."

"Sounds good. Wash your filthy paws when you're done if you're sharing my hummus."

They could hear a set of footsteps approaching, and Jack scrambled to the door to help Noah lean against it. The man turned the knob, and seemed to struggle trying to open it. There was such a lack of physical effort at first that Jack thought the man might give up and just not come in… but then he started slamming against it.

And he was huge.

The door came open and Noah fell backwards, sliding across the floor on his backside. Jack backed away into the darkness, watching as the tall man in the rabbit mask entered. Noah could barely see Jack back there now, and he wondered if he would just save his own skin and leave Noah to be beaten to a pulp by this monster of a guy. He could tell that his head was shaved bald, and he had a full beard beneath the mask. He was as wide as the opening of the door, and tall enough that he had to duck to get in.

"What the fuck are you doing in here?" he asked Noah, advancing towards him and still unaware of Jack.

"I.. I'm just… I'm lost," Noah babbled, whistling through his broken teeth.

The man looked behind Noah at the redheaded woman laying in the corner, and Noah winced before the man ever spoke.

"What is that? What the fuck! Is she dead?" the man's voice was a cross between anger and shrill horror.

"It's a long story," Noah started.

"Oh, when I get done with you…"

Jack raised the gun and Noah looked at him. The man noticed Noah's eyes move and focus somewhere behind him, and he slowly turned. The rabbit's silver and white face glistened, sparkling in the dim light. The man's eyes widened in surprise only a moment before Jack fired.

The man stumbled, but did not fall, although Jack had shot him right between the eyes. There was no exit wound that Noah could see from behind. The man wavered on his feet, but put his arms out like a mummy that was coming for his victim, and Jack fired again.

This shot went through a portion of the man's eye, and he fell straight backwards, stiff as a board. Noah could not believe how quickly the man had died. He didn't know anything about guns, but he had underestimated just how effortlessly lethal they could be.

"Jack!" Noah said, voice rising in pitch.

Jack ignored him, tucking the gun into his waistband as he stalked over to the table in the corner, shuffling through the sex toys and other items in the black bag. Noah watched in stunned silence as Jack retrieved a silver folding knife from within. He spent seconds examining it, turning it over in his bruised hands, then tucked it into his pocket, producing the stolen lighter in turn.

"What are you doing?" Noah asked.

"Getting out of here." Jack said, clambering up to hold the lighter up to a sprinkler, letting the flame lick the little wheel of metal until…

Lights flashed on, and in the hallway they could see that they were pulsing. Water sprayed down from the ceilings, and an alarm sounded: the forlorn wail of a siren that made Noah's head want to explode. Water pooled on the rabbit man's eye sockets, making little pitter-pattering puddles.

19

JACK COULD NOT CALM his pounding heart as the two of them stalked down the red hall and back into the waiting room where they'd been given the menus. The couch was saturated with water from the sprinklers now. There was a single door that lay between them and the lobby where their wallets and phones were stored inside the ticket booth.

Just as they reached the door, Jack heard someone coming down the hall. Their feet made sloshing sounds in the gathering water, the man with the bear mask making a bee-line for them. When he walked his arms swung like they were giant pendulums.

Noah dove for the door to the lobby, turning it so hard that he opened the wound on his palm, smearing crust and a stringy clot onto the bronze surface.

Jack drew the gun back out of his pants, shooting at the man in the flashing light of the hallway. He missed, and the man ducked, taking the chance to try and rush him before he had an opportunity to fire again.

The second shot struck him in the throat, and the third split his chin in half: two pieces of jaw separating at the seam and dangling on either side of his burst tongue as he collapsed onto the floor. Jack was so glad he had used that gift card to the shooting range, and that his wife had continued to buy him range time every year for his birthday and Christmas. He thought he would probably never have a need to use a gun, and he never carried one. A handgun sat in his closet in a safe that he didn't even remember the combination to anymore. He hadn't even been sure he would have been able to use it on an intruder in his home, had there been one.

Noah managed to get the door open behind him, and was running into the lobby. Jack had a twinge of excitement and relief in his gut, exhaustion falling even heavier on him as he came closer to escape.

A woman ran out from behind the counter, and he recognized her as the one who had given them their shirts and taken their wallets. Jack immediately raised the gun to kill her as well. She put her hands into the air, stopping dead still in the middle of the room.

"No, please!" she said, but Jack stood firm. She was one of them, and she would take them out if she had the chance. She'd throw them to the wolves, sell out their families. This was just another sacrifice that Jack was willing to make. He would not leave anyone alive, if he had the chance. He would not risk anyone coming after him.

"Close your eyes," Jack said quietly, voice cracking.

The woman pursed her lips together, arms shaking as she continued to hold them up but she did close her eyes. They fluttered shut, tears forced down her cheeks. Jack waited a few seconds, giving her the chance to take a deep breath, to stop anticipating. He imagined the shot, the course the bullet would take into her brain, forcing tissue away as it embedded itself deep within and left a trail of heat and soot and ruin.

Noah lunged at him the moment that he squeezed the trigger, shoving his arm up into the air as the shot fired. It buried itself in the building's structure with a thump. The woman dove down, scampering out the front door and running screaming through the parking lot.

Jack turned around slowly, glaring at Noah who was standing

there with tears running down his face again. He had his hands pressed together like someone praying. Jack had never felt such a rage, such pure hatred for someone he had once loved like a brother.

"Please, Jack. No more killing. No one else. I can't live with myself, I can't handle any more of this. Please, please, please..."

He didn't have to, he recognized at that moment. He didn't *have* to shoot Noah. *He wanted to.* So he did. He raised the gun, shooting his friend in the face as he bowed before him. He saw the slit of tissue on Noah's cheek start to pour dark blood, and when Noah spun away Jack shot him again through the neck. Noah turned towards him, eyes heavy with some kind of emotion that Jack had never witnessed before: unfiltered and raw desolation and anguish.

Noah clutched at the wound on the back of his neck, clamping his hand over it like he had been stung by a bee and was trying to smash it. Even as blood continued to pour out of his face, and the star-shaped exit wound near his throat. He slumped first onto his knees, and Jack dropped down to cradle the back of his head and lay him down onto the floor.

"Shhhhh," Jack hissed, patting him on the chest as he let him rest on the floor.

Noah grappled for his shirt with shaking hands, "No, please, hold me. Please just hold me, don't leave me here."

Jack was surprised that Noah didn't ask him why, like they did in the movies during a betrayal. He thought that maybe it was because Noah knew he deserved it. Jack settled onto the ground, pulling Noah into his lap like he had the blonde backstage. Water from the sprinklers washed away the blood from Noah's face, diluting it on the floor.

"I knew we wouldn't make it..." Noah said, managing to smile somehow, although blood stained and pulsed between his shattered teeth. Jack briefly reached up to pinch off the frazzled end of Noah's right jugular as it deposited copious amounts of blood onto his lap. "I saw it all, and this is it, I've been laying here and seeing it all happen again but this is it. Here I am again, back here. This is it."

"Sorry," Jack said simply, looking down at him. "I can't risk going out there with you. I have to get out of here. Do you understand?"

Noah's body tremored and he started to cry again. "My house key is in the ceramic frog's mouth."

"I'll feed the cat," Jack promised, and he meant it.

Noah seemed satisfied with this, taking a shaky breath as he stared off into some other place beyond this one. He was still breathing, this ragged kind of short huff over and over again. It made his lower lip flutter in and out, chest bobbing with the effort. Jack let him slip onto the floor and he went into the ticket booth, retrieving all of their wallets. He tucked them fondly into his pockets, and hid the gun back into his waistband. It was empty. He had thought that it may have been when he had fired the first shot at Noah, and then the second but it had continued to reciprocate. The slide was locked back now, signaling it finally had nothing else to give.

Noah's body was still and quiet now, just a thing in the middle of the floor. A hull, a shell, something unimportant shed away. Jack lifted him under the arms and dragged him over behind the ticket booth, finding that there was a series of small square screens underneath the lip of the desk. They all provided grainy images of the hallways around the building, and the now-empty parking lot.

Jack could see a figure coming up the main hall, straight towards the lobby where he stood. It was a woman, and he could tell by the way she walked that it was Vixxn. He ducked down behind the counter.

20

Vixxn walked briskly through the parking lot, digging for her keyfob in her purse. She pointed it at the line of cars, pressing the button several times in a row until she saw the flashing headlights and heard the high-pitched beeping of her vehicle. Her phone rang and she paused long enough to answer, "Yes?"

"Hey, Vee. We got two of the guys, and we're on the other one. We'll have it taken care of and get the cleanup crew in before next weekend."

"Great. Let me know when it's handled."

"There's a little bit of an issue though," he said, voice unsteady.

"What's that?"

"Well, did you go out the lobby?"

Vixxn scoffed, "No, I left out the back. Why? *Spit it out.*"

"So there's the one guy, the one the dogs got, you know. We've got that mess all cleaned up. Then the second guy, we found him in the lobby, shot twice. We also got two of our guys dead from gunshot wounds too."

Vixxn was quiet for several moments. She didn't allow guns in the establishment for obvious reasons. Tensions were always high.

Hell, *everyone was always high*. There were cleaner, easier ways to dispose of a troublemaker: dogs, knives, blunt force, overdose.

"Who did it?"

"We don't know yet."

"The last guy?"

"No, we're on his trail. Probably not him, especially since whoever it was shot the friend too. We're on it. We'll get it figured out. Don't worry about it."

"Oh, I'm going to worry about it. Deal with it *now*."

She hung up.

What a shitshow, what an absolute *shitshow*.

She stopped in her tracks as she heard a thump to her left. Something that sounded like metal on metal, a clunk against the hood of a car. An alarm started going off on a red van. She straightened her spine, heading towards the van as it screamed in the night. She approached the backside, noticing the Heresy County license plate and the bumper stickers which indicated the driver had a family with children and a dog, someone was a proud EMT, proud dance mom, and 'Do You Follow Jesus This Close?'.

Vixxn rounded the side of the van. She didn't see anyone, but there was a black gun on the ground, and a shining dent on the hood of the vehicle.

Vixxn reached down and picked up the handgun, noting from the position of the slide that it had been depleted. It was a .45, all metal. She dropped it back to the ground, looking around the empty lot. There were only a handful of cars left including hers, most belonging to patrons who wouldn't make it back out. She had an eerie, creeping feeling like someone may have been watching her. She crept back around the side of the van first, looking in the direction where she thought the gun may have been thrown from. There was no one there. A breeze blew the leaves in the trees that bordered the parking lot. In the distance she could hear the faint sound of a train. The night air was crisp, and only served to intensify the chill on her spine.

Vixxn set her jaw and hurried on to her car.

She jumped into the seat so heavily that the car rocked, locking the doors immediately as she leaned to look out the windshield again. Nothing. The night was still and quiet, a dusky haze covering the gravel lot and her prized building. She noticed the alarm and lights had finally gone off, and everything inside was still and dark.

Vixxn started the car, tossing her purse and phone into the passenger seat. The dash dinged an alert at her persistently. She sighed in frustration and buckled up, but the alarm continued to sound. Brow furrowing, she checked the dash lights. Gas level was good, tire levels good.

REAR DRIVER'S SIDE DOOR AJAR.

Vixxn froze, slowly sitting until her back was against the seat, eyes flicking up to the rearview mirror.

She saw the silhouette of a man with a beaked mask sitting quietly behind her, a blade shimmering gently in his hand. Vixxn had never been a screamer, she didn't think she had it in her to scream.

However, as the man lunged over the back of the seat, slitting her throat and coating her windshield with a spray of erubescent arterial blood, she did *try* to do just that.

ABOUT THE EDITOR / PUBLISHER

Dawn Shea is an author and half of the publishing team over at D&T Publishing. She lives with her family in Mississippi. Always an avid horror lover, she has moved forward with her dreams of writing and publishing those things she loves so much.

D&T Previously published material:
    ABC's of Terror
    After the Kool-Aid is Gone

Follow her author page on Amazon for all publications she is featured in.
    Follow D&T Publishing at the following locations:
    Website
    Facebook: Page / Group
    Or email us here: dandtpublishing20@gmail.com

MEGAN STOCKTON

Megan Stockton is an indie author who lives in Grimsley Tennessee with her two children and her husband, who is an indie filmmaker. She writes in a variety of genres that all have dark/horror elements, and all of her work is character-driven and immersive. She is known for delivering works that are raw, thought-provoking, brutal, and cinematic. She has been writing since she was a child and was always obsessed with horror and the macabre. When she isn't writing (or working her day job) she likes to work with the animals on their farm, read, play video games, and watch movies.

Bluejay by Megan Stockton

Edited by Patrick C. Harrison III

Cover by Ash Ericmore

Formatting by J.Z. Foster

Bluejay by Megan Stockton

Made in the USA
Middletown, DE
09 October 2023

40504180R00062